AJAY KHANNA

Tangled in 1984

a novel

Cover design by Peter Selgin

First edition

ISBN: 979-8-9897721-0-0

*This book was professionally typeset on Reedsy.
Find out more at reedsy.com*

Contents

asato mā sadgamaya,
tamaso mā jyotirgamaya,
mrtyormā'mrtam gamaya.

From ignorance lead me to the truth,
From darkness lead me to light,
From death lead me to immortality.

—Brihadaranyaka Upanishad

1

Independence Day

It was the year 2007. The August sun shone bright, its rays
bathing Fremont in warm light. It was not uncommon for the
California city, where most days are sunny and bright. Over
the years, the town became a hub for the Indian community
of the Bay Area. Though not quite 8:00 a.m., Chetan Malhotra
was already at Lake Elizabeth, where the *mela*, a big carnival,
was being set up.

Chetan was a man in his mid-thirties with light brown skin,
or what they call "wheatish" in India. His brown eyes were
hidden behind his eyeglasses. His mother would tease him
about his small eyes.

Are you trying to be angry? I cannot tell from your tiny eyes, she
would say and laugh at him.

His black curly hair was cut short. Gray showed at the sides,
though. He would not color his hair and never believed he had
to hide his age to look a certain way. It was a Saturday, so he
had not shaved. He never shaved on weekends. Chetan was
about six feet tall, but one could not tell because of his habit
of waking with a slight hunch and drooping shoulders. Very

unlike the Punjabi boy that he was.

The crowd amassed. People were taking their places along-side the road well before the start of the event so they could get the best view. Many brought their garden chairs and set them up on the roadside, some spread mats on the ground, and a few just sat on the sidewalk. Chetan cautiously walked around the park with a blue camping chair hanging on his shoulder.

The India Day parade, meant to celebrate Indian indepen-dence from British rule in 1947, was to start in a couple of hours. India got its freedom from the empire on August 15, 1947, when the British finally left India, but the scars of the imperial atrocities stayed with the country and its people for a long time.

This was August 18, but holding celebrations over the week-end was more convenient for the organizers and participants. Interestingly, Indo-Americans decided to organize the parade for Independence Day and not for Republic Day, January 26, when India actually has the annual parade. More than sixty thousand people from all over the San Francisco Bay Area were expected to flock to the streets of Fremont to watch it.

Many came to see the grand marshal, usually a Bollywood actor. The Indian diaspora in the Bay Area was strong, and they raised enough money to get some A-listers from the tinsel town of Mumbai. Previously, heavyweights such as Urmila Matondkar, Sunil Shetty, and many other superstars had graced the occasion. This year, as well, a top actor was expected to join. But Chetan was not interested in meeting the Bollywood stars. Large gatherings made him nervous, however, he still visited the parade every year.

Chetan found some comfort in the presence of officers from the Fremont Police Department, who had already taken their positions at the designated spots. There were about twenty police cars scattered along the length of Paseo Padre Parkway in case there was any unexpected violence. A few police officers with bomb-sniffing dogs randomly inspected parked vehicles. Half a dozen police motorcycles were making rounds up and down along Paseo Padre Parkway, where the procession took place every year.

Chetan nervously scanned all the activities around him. Preparations for the *mela* were in full force. Vendors had set up their stalls along the sides—the usual Indian food and handicrafts. The tea stall was already seeing some lines. The dosa vendor was setting up the equipment. There were stalls for mouthwatering chaats, aromatic biryanis, and snacks, including samosa, jalebi, and gulab jamun. The aroma of delectable Indian cuisine wafted through the air, drawing everyone toward the numerous food stalls set up under white makeshift tents.

Chetan watched as many NGOs put up their banners and decorated their stations. The day of the parade was one of the most significant fundraising events. Social organizations used this opportunity to raise awareness about their initiatives, ranging from promoting Indian culture and art to providing assistance to those in need. Their causes varied from promoting child education, providing shelter for orphaned children, and supporting widows to providing free eye clinics to the less fortunate in India. There were booths displaying large banners to promote yoga and save Indian culture.

Promote yoga? Chetan thought. *Does it need any more promotion? Every twenty-four-hour fitness center has four classes a week, and the city has two dozen other yoga studios.*

A smirk played on Chetan's lips at the sight of the growing

queue before the samosa stall. The vibrant energy of the crowd intrigued him, their animated conversations punctuated by the occasional burst of laughter. He couldn't wrap his mind around the idea of indulging in samosas this early in the morning. It seemed absurd to him. Samosas were always an evening tea snack, at least from where he came. Jalebi and samosa are the quintessential Punjabi evening tea menu items. Chetan's favorite breakfast was fried egg over buttered toast. He walked from stall to stall, nodding to people setting up their booths, smiling to some, and gesturing with a slight bow of his head, offering his humble wishes.

He had more than an hour to spend before the parade crossed Lake Elizabeth. He stopped by the free health check booth and got his height, weight, and blood pressure measured. The lady in the booth asked him to read the eye charts for far and near sight, and went on to complete his health report.

"Your BMI is twenty-six. You should try to lose ten pounds," the woman said as she handed Chetan his report.

He nodded and smiled. He had been lanky all his life. He was not particularly athletic, but he surely did not need to lose ten pounds.

"Thank you." He folded the report and slid it into his pocket as he walked toward the stall serving free Starbucks coffee.

As Chetan walked along the park with coffee in his hand, he admired hundreds of Indian national flags, *Tiranga* – the tricolor, fluttering alongside the road. Horizontal rectangular flags with saffron, white, and green colors and a blue Ashoka Chakra – 24-spoke wheel – in the center added a remarkable color to the otherwise bland street. Spectators lined up on the street, waving flags of various sizes and waiting for the procession to pass by. Families, friends, and people from different walks of life came together to celebrate their roots and connect with their shared cultural identity. Children excitedly held mini flags while elderly community members gossiped in groups or cared for their grandchildren.

The performance stage was set up, where some children and women practiced their dance performances to showcase the diverse cultural heritage of India. Crowds were now amassing quickly, and Chetan sped his way to his spot. The loudspeakers played an old patriotic song, "*Aao Bachcho Tumhain Dekhain Jhanki Hindustan Ki.*" Chetan smiled and shook his head. He was never one of the patriotic kinds who would wear emotions on his sleeve, but he had attended this parade yearly since 1999.

The parade began at the Paseo Padre Parkway and Capital Avenue crossing, and it would take twenty-five minutes for the first float to arrive at Lake Elizabeth. Chetan pulled out the camping chair from its carry bag and sat with his back to the lake, comfortably sipping his coffee. He looked at the row of houses across the street with the lake view. The houses, each with a balcony overlooking the lake, were neatly lined across the road. Each residence boasted panoramic views of the glistening lake, adorned with charming gardens that whispered tales of a peaceful suburban retreat. A few of them had older people sitting on their balconies, sipping their tea or coffee and waiting for this annual spectacle. Chetan wondered about the house prices in that area and whether he could afford such a house. Probably not.

It's called a home, not a house., a voice in his head corrected him.

He nodded. *Yes, a home.*

The first float of the parade had just appeared. In the front were two young men in their early twenties. Chetan's cynical mind assumed they must be sons of some city socialites or some start-up CEOs who donated to the parade. They were each holding a flag and waving it vigorously. One had the US Stars and Stripes, and the other had India's *Tiranga*. This year, the plan was to have the grand marshal lead a caravan of one hundred cars and more than two dozen floats representing various Indian states, local temples, and some not-for-profit organizations. Volunteers from multiple groups and clubs across the Bay Area had converted flatbed trucks into floats and colorfully decorated them. It was supposed to be the biggest parade that northern California had ever seen.

Organizations representing various states brought their floats, or tableaux as they were called in India. Rajasthan, Andhra, Tamil Nadu, Gujarat, and all other states were duly represented. The first float was shaped like a peacock, India's national bird. Many floats were decorated as palaces, some as temples, and Uttar Pradesh's float was the quintessential Taj Mahal.

Amateurish quality, Chetan thought.

Men with *dhols*, the Indian drums, around their necks accompanied the peacock float. They wore Nehru caps on their head, a tricolor sash across their chests, and big red tilak on their foreheads. Their puffed chests and their attempts at synchronized marching amused Chetan. Twelve women were on top of the float, another six on each side, posing in different Indian classical dance mudras, or forms.

The excitement ran high—as did the hopes of Indians in 1947.

Rallying cries filled the air.

"Bharat Mata ki Jai!" Victory for Mother India.

"Hindustan Zindabad!" Long live India.

"Jai Hind!" Victory to India.

The crowd along the stretch of road was in the thousands, and the noise of slogans was deafening. Chetan's eyes cautiously scanned each float. As soon as the *Cadillac Convertible* with the grand marshal appeared, his head turned toward another group of about seventy-five people across the street.

Amid the jubilant festivities of the Indian Independence Day parade, a somber undertone was brought forth by a small group of people with grim faces. They did not seem to be enjoying the festivities around them. The ones with the black flags. The protesters. The group had people of all ages, including young boys and girls and their old grandparents, holding placards and banners with scathing messages demanding justice and accountability from the Indian government. Many were wearing their turbans, primarily black. Half a dozen police officers flanked them with their hands on their batons. As the grand marshal's car came near the group, it erupted.

"Down with the terrorist state!"

"Bring us justice!"

"Shame on India!"

"Hang the 1984 killers!"

"Jo Bole So Nihal, Sat Sri Akaal!"

The commotion became Thunderous. A protester ensured the group stayed staying behind the temporary metal barriers. As long as they stayed put, the police would not have any issues with their protest. Another police officer crossed the crowd on a motorcycle, signaling with the hand to remain behind the barricade.

Protesters made every attempt to embarrass the grand marshal, a movie actor. He was greeted with the piercing

"*Hai, hai*" slogans and "Shame on you." There were calls to boycott his movies. The actor did not look at that side and just waved to the friendlier crowd on the opposite side of the street. Clearly, the organizers had prepared him for the sequence of the events.

Chetan's heart beat faster, and anxiety permeated his body. He felt as if blood was draining out of his cheeks, and a side of his face was getting numb. He stood there frozen and tried hard not to reveal his emotions. However, the more he tried to suppress his feelings, the stronger they got and transported him into another world. A world that he wanted to forget about.

Chetan's thoughts were interrupted by a person standing next to him. The middle-aged male wore a white kurta, green pants, and orange Modi jacket—he was dressed as patriotic as possible. He attempted to have a conversation with Chetan.

"Why do these people come and protest here every year? Why don't the police drive them away?"

Chetan glanced at him and shrugged. "Don't know. Free country, you know."

Chetan knew very well why those people were there. He had been with them. He grew up with them.

Their voices became louder as floats drove in front of them, as if there was a competition – no, not a competition, a war between the black and tricolor flag bearers. With each passing float, the passions kept rising. Anger in the voices and bloodthirsty eyes made the police cautious. Their radios crackled with commands, and the grips on their batons tightened. Officers exchanged wary glances, each one acutely aware of the potential for the situation to escalate. The protesters were just a thin line of barricades away from the parade route, and the anxiety among the officers was palpable.

The shouting became more animated, fists punched the air, and the barriers were rattling. The protesters were impassioned and determined to ensure their message was heard loud and clear.

A group of ladies started screaming.

"Hindustan, *hai, hai*."

"*Hai. hai.*"

"India kills minorities."

With each shout of "*Hai, hai*," they slapped their chests harder and harder, their pain evident in their screams.

An old lady caught Chetan's attention. She must have been over eighty. She was short, with a hunched back, wearing a white *salwar* and *kameez* with a black *dupatta* carefully covering her head. The attire of mourning. She seemed familiar, and maybe she was here last year as well. There was a quivering pain in her voice. Chetan could feel it. His ears were isolating her screams from the other voices of dissonance. Few teardrops escaped her eyes, but her voice was firm and loud. Even with her throwing her hands in the air with each "Bring us justice" or beating of her chest on "*Hai, hai*," the *dupatta* covering her head never moved an inch. Like a security cover, a cover protecting her honor. Chetan was wondering: *How did it stay there?*

The tricolor people were not going to take this lying down. Their voices went louder and louder, trying to drown protests.

"*Hindustan zindabad!*"

"*Bharat mata ki jai!*"

"*Jai Hind!*"

Amid the chaos, Chetan's eyes locked onto a young woman who conveyed a remarkable tranquility. She had a tray with a dozen paper cups filled with steaming hot chai. She was there making rounds from a table she had set on the roadside to the passing parade, as well as the protesters standing behind the barricade. She did not look worried and did not seem to take sides. Instead, she was busy going back and forth from her table, filling more cups, and serving chai.

She looked to be around Chetan's age. She wore a yellow kurta over blue denim jeans and had covered her head with a sky-blue *dupatta*. It was an odd way to dress, but it had become commonplace in the Bay Area. Bringing the East and West together or a marriage of convenience. She was committed to her *seva*, her duty, insisting that people pick a cup of chai.

Amid the spew of violent slogans, she had the strength and calmness of a dam that appeared to keep the two sides separate. It seemed if she were not here, the two groups would have leaped at each other and torn each other apart.

Every Independence Day parade, Chetan watched her serving chai to both sides. As the event grew over the years, so did her stock. This year, she had over a dozen hot tea dispensers ready. A glance at her would bring a sense of serenity to the most agitated mind. Chetan visited the parade every year just to watch her smile as she served people and offered chai.

The coffee had cooled to lukewarm now. Chetan put the cup down, sliding it under his folding chair so no one would kick and spill it. He checked the time. It was almost eleven. His eyes were now rapidly moving, scanning the crowds, their belongings, and the slightest sudden movements. It was the kind of area sweep one would expect Secret Service members to do behind their dark glasses. Crowds made him uneasy, and this compulsion of intentionally trying to find something wrong in every situation had become an annoyance he had struggled with for many years. He would always find himself in a conundrum of worst-case scenarios. Yet, every year, here he was, fighting his fears.

As Chetan surveyed the crowd, his eyes stopped at a middle-aged man standing among the protesters. The man with a brown-colored backpack hanging on his back. He was not shouting slogans but standing quietly, leaning on a tree with both hands in his pockets. He had a full-grown beard but was not wearing the turban, like most other protesting men. Instead, he had his head covered with a saffron-colored cloth. He was not screaming slogans like others, and Chetan wondered why. Chetan looked at the other people standing next to him. He hoped someone would speak to this person. He wanted to ensure that this person had company and was not some loner.

Does anyone know him? Did he come alone?

Why are his hands in his pockets?

What is inside that backpack?

A series of thoughts engulfed his mind. His mind was racing like a bullet train. Sudden fight or flight instincts kicked in. He searched for escape paths and calculated his distance from the person. He checked out the nearest policeman.

How far could the impact go?

Should I alert the police?

Why are they not checking his backpack?

But there was a metal detector at the entrance. Chetan's mind raced.

So, we have nothing to worry about.

What if he snuck in from the back road and jumped the fences?

His heart pounded. He put his fingers on his wrist. His pulse was high, one twenty, one thirty. He whispered to himself.

11

"It's just in my head. It's just in my head."

"Breathe."

"Breathe in 1 . . . 2 . . . 3 . . . 4 . . . 5 . . ."

"Hold 1 . . . 2 . . . 3 . . . 4 . . . 5 . . ."

"Breathe out 1 . . . 2 . . . 3 . . . 4 . . . 5 . . ."

Chetan continued his breathing exercises with his fingers on his wrist. He tried to look away from that person, hoping that the feeling would disappear if he somehow could find a way to ignore him. He thought of walking up to him just to say hello. Maybe that would ease his fear. But he could not muster the courage. Courage was not something that came naturally to him. He was just hoping that the person would simply disappear or for cops to take him away.

It felt like something was wringing his heart. A vise squeezing it hard. His breaths were shallow. His arms were overpowered with a debilitating numbing and tingling sensation. It felt like he was getting a heart attack and would collapse anytime now.

Chetan tried to take control of the situation. He did not want to scream or cry lest he embarrass himself again. A trip to the emergency room would have been sure if this had happened a few years back. He had made more than a few trips to the ER, but now he knew what it was and learned how to manage it. Chetan had learned to identify the onset of panic attacks. He had had them for as long as he could remember.

The Independence Day parade in Fremont proceeded without any incident. The protesters continued their slogans, and the floats kept on moving. Chetan kept his eye on the man with the backpack. The man moved toward the barracks and grabbed a cup of tea.

He is not here for any trouble. Chetan told himself. *He is picking tea, just like the others. If he meant harm, he would not walk all the way to grab tea—another false alarm.*

Chetan kept reminding himself to calm down until his pulse came back to normal. He despised himself for these thoughts.

Why do I not have the courage like others, and why am I always so scared?

I guess I was brought up that way, to be afraid.

He continued his breathing exercises, feet flat on the ground, holding his breath, fingers on his wrist, and thought about how this all began.

2

New Year's Eve, December 1983

Chetan was ten and a half years old and at home in Patiala, a small but vibrant city nestled in the heart of the state of Punjab. With its storied history dating back to the eighteenth century, Patiala exuded an air of regal splendor, evident in its magnificent palaces and awe-inspiring architecture. The city was known for its royal history, fantastic food, and excellent educational institutions.

Chetan's family, the Malhotras–Punjabi Hindus, had recently moved into this house in Patiala. They rented this place after Chetan's father, Vijay, got promoted to deputy manager from a senior engineer position. They could afford a bigger rental home. It was a sizeable three-bedroom house on the ground floor of a two-story house. His mother, Renu, was very excited about this new place. The house had a bigger kitchen, a large drawing room, and bedrooms with attached bathrooms. The owners occupied the upper floor. Chetan and his younger brother, Vikas, or Vikki as everyone called him, got their own rooms. Vikki was about three years younger than Chetan but was his constant companion. This was the first time they started sleeping alone. Chetan was scared for the first few days. Having Vikki sleeping next to him used to give him some sense of comfort and security. Sleeping alone in a dark room still required getting used to. Chetan's father, Vijay, bought him a nightlight for his room, and Chetan would stare at the dim red hue of the bulb till he fell asleep. It took a while for Chetan to get used to a separate room, although he enjoyed having his own closet and walls to affix Elton John and Ivan Lendl posters. The TV stayed in the parents' bedroom, so they had complete control over what to watch and when to watch it. The house came with a big lawn on the side and a nice backyard that was paved with bricks. Most of the evenings were spent within the house's perimeter, but it had enough space to play tennis-ball cricket or sometimes run around on roller skates along the cemented driveway.

The owners, a Randhawa Sikh family, were very welcoming to the Malhotras. Chetan's Mom soon became good friends with the landlady, and they would spend afternoons together basking in the winter sun, knitting sweaters, and exchanging designs. Mrs. Randhawa was a tall woman, towering Chetan's mother. Her imposing, heavy build and somewhat hoarse voice made her intimidating. Chetan avoided her for the first few weeks after they moved in. Only on the continuous insistence of Mrs. Randhawa's son, who was the same age as Chetan, did he go upstairs to their house. Mrs. Randhawa was not particularly religious, but one could call her a woman of faith and strongheaded at that. If she brought up any discussion on the current political climate or the militancy, Chetan's mother would not get involved and would change the topic. Renu was always tactful and knew how to handle such conversations without getting entangled in heated debates.

15

The situation in the state of Punjab was grim. The state assembly was recently dissolved, and the president's rule was imposed on the state. The police were given unprecedented powers, but the killings by insurgents continued. Every day, there was some or other news about shoot-outs, bombings, kidnappings, riots, and clashes. Newspapers kept the tally of killings and published counts of Hindus, Sikhs, and policemen killed, diligently classifying the body count according to religion, age, and gender in the states of Haryana and Punjab. Luckily, Patiala was not in the red zone, and in spite of all the ruckus across the state, the city was relatively untroubled, but everyone kept a vigil.

At home, parents regularly reminded kids about what not to say in public and trained them to be vigilant. Religious discussions were particularly forbidden. The school followed the regular schedule: Vikki was picked up by the rickshaw every morning at seven-thirty and dropped home at two in the evening. Chetan drove his bicycle to school. The school walls were made higher and retrofitted with large twenty-foot gates. The gates were locked at eight-thirty sharp. If you were late to school, you were turned back. School was usually the only time Chetan and Vikki were allowed to step out of the house. Chetan missed playing out with his friends and going shopping at the bazaar, but he understood that the times were not good. He was afraid to go out of the house in the evenings. He spent most of his evenings inside the house, working on homework, reading comic books, or painting. It had been over a year since the family even went to the Kali Mandir or the Modi Mandir temples. They used to go to one of those temples every Tuesday.

This year, there was no Dussehra festival and no *Ram-Leela*

16

performance on the grounds of the Modi Mandir temple. That annual celebration was shelved a couple of years back. Fewer people had been visiting the temple, and the collections were not enough to support the extravagant burning of Ravana's effigy. Moreover, no one would risk bringing in crowds and inciting violence on the holy grounds.

Chetan remembered the last time he visited Ravana Dahan was in 1981. His father took him and Vikki to watch the final day of *Ram-Leela*, the annual enactment of Ramayana that went on for twenty days. The finale of *Ram-Leela* was followed by the torching of a huge forty-foot Ravana that eventually would collapse amid the loud fireworks. Vikki sat atop their father's shoulders, too short to see the scene from the ground. After the fall of Ravana, they ran toward it to grab a burning wooden stick, a part of the frame around which Ravana's effigy was built. It was said that if you could bury that stick in front of the house, it would ward off the evil spirits. But that was in the past.

Chetan couldn't even get firecrackers to celebrate Diwali that year. Firecrackers were banned so that no one mistook a firecracker boom for some bomb explosion. Even decorating the house with lighted candles was deemed dangerous, lest it offend someone. With so much mourning, sadness, and fear, people were not in the mood to decorate or celebrate. The Diwali celebration was restricted to puja inside the house and some special dinner with the family. When Chetan's Dad felt bold enough, he would let him and Vikki light some sparklers in the backyard. Away from the public eye. What's Diwali without the firecrackers and lighting candles?

Festivals had lost their luster, their meaning. No celebration of the victory of good over evil, light over darkness, no clouds

17

of color and water balloon fights on Holi, and no visiting family on Rakshabandhan. It was as if a strange dark spirit had engulfed everyone's lives and isolated people from one another. Everyone was cautious, jittery, looking over their shoulders, and suspicious of everyone all the time. Chetan, his brother, and the whole generation growing up in this turmoil had cynicism and mistrust ingrained in their psyche.

Chetan took these things especially hard. He often asked his parents, "Why can't we celebrate Diwali or Holi like other people on TV?" The rest of India seemed to celebrate all the festivals with full pomp and splendor, but Punjab remained dark and gloomy.

"Why can't we visit Chacha Ji?"

"Why can't we go to Ferozepur to visit Mama Ji?" Chetan would plead. But the responses from his father never varied. Buses were not safe. Travel was not safe. The crowds were not safe. Going to the movies was not safe. Driving at night was not safe.

People used to keep celebrations low-key. This year, Chetan and his family were not venturing out to celebrate New Year's Eve. Chetan loved the annual party at the famed Maharani Club. This venerable institution was more than just a recreational space; it was a sanctuary of camaraderie and sophistication where the city's elite gathered for a game of billiards or poker over scotch and fish fry. While its grandeur and allure remained undiminished over the years, the turbulent period of the 1980s cast a shadow of caution upon the club and its patrons. A place that was once a vibrant symbol of the city's affluence looked like a guarded prison. To enter the Maharani Club, even on a routine day, one had to tread through the labyrinth of security checkpoints and

18

roadblocks, always under the watchful eye of armed personnel. This year, the club did not organize any party. Authorities strongly advised people not to venture out after dark. Chetan stayed home with his family.

It was the late evening of December 31 1983, and Chetan, Vikki, and their parents were home, getting ready to watch the New Year's program on the national TV channel, the Delhi Doordarshan. The program was to celebrate the year passing by and welcome the incoming year 1984. There was no cable and not much choice of channels either. In Patiala, their TV antenna would sometimes catch the signal from Jalandhar Doordarshan, but not very often. The whole family was looking forward to the program.

Chetan's mother cooked dinner early so she would not have to bother with the kitchen work after the program had started. The New Year's Eve dinner at home had to be something special. Mom did not cook the regular dal, sabzi, and roti but made everyone's favorite snacks. She had prepared mixed pakoras—potato, cauliflower, mushrooms, brinjal, and paneer fritters. The vegetables used to be seasonal, and everyone eagerly awaited gobi's arrival in winter—the cauliflower. The first few times, it would taste out of this world, and then toward the weaning end of winter, no one would give it a second look.

Chetan was in and out of the kitchen and could not wait to get his hands on some of those, but he did not pick any from the kitchen. He did not want to annoy his mother, as the repercussions could be dire. It was best to wait until she brought those out for dinner. Chetan's father had bought freshly roasted peanuts and an assortment of gajak and rewari for the family to munch until the clock struck midnight. It was a staple pastime during the winter season. Chetan's dad had a favorite shop at 22 No. Phatak market, where he would buy the fresh peanuts roasted in front of him and bring those home while they were still warm. The 22 No. Phatak market was named after the railway crossing number that bordered one end of the shopping row, and the place had become a legend in its own right. After pakoras, peanuts, and gajak, a few rounds of chai would keep them awake through the scheduled program.

The family gathered on the bed in front of the black-and-white Konark TV at 9:00 p.m., right after *Samachar*, the Hindi news. The color transmission started in 1982 when India hosted the Asian Games, but colored TVs were far from mainstream. The color on Chetan's TV screen was due to a protective front cover that had blue hues on the top and green at the bottom.

Chetan and his family were tucked inside heavy *razais*, the comforters filled with cotton that was taken out, fluffed and refilled every winter. The room heater on the floor hummed and emanated the smell of burning plastic.

The room lights were turned off. The program was being watched at a low volume, and the dim light from the TV flickered shadows on the walls. Chetan's parents, who had lived through the war of 1965, had instinctively shut the house lights off. Though not at war now, Punjab was going through a strained and dangerous period. Chetan's parents kept the lights off not due to the fear of airstrikes but because open celebrations of any kind were frowned upon and could rub miscreants the wrong way. They wanted to be careful. Sitting in the dark added to the drama and fear; the slightest sound would startle Chetan. Chetan was on high alert. Any noise from outside would make him tiptoe toward the window. He would move the curtain just slightly to see what was happening outside. The family kept a field hockey stick, cricket bat, or a screwdriver close by, as if they had any chance if a person with a Kalashnikov AK-47 came knocking at their door.

The TV variety program was underway. Short comedy sketches were followed by a series of singers and some dance performances. The show was graced by beloved personalities and featured dazzling performances by Bollywood stars, captivating dance routines, and heartwarming musical numbers. However, the classical dances and singing would put everyone off.

The listless performance irritated Renu. "Why on this night? They have the whole year to sing their classical ragas," she commented.

"You can do disco with it if you like," Vijay quipped.

"Why don't you do it, and we all will watch?"

The kids laughed at their parents' pretend fight. They loved seeing this banter between Mom and Dad. So, the section with classical recitals was used as a bathroom break or to run to the kitchen, dump the peanut shells, and grab another pile. Mom left for the kitchen to make another round of chai.

The program continued. Midnight loomed. They all were ready to wish each other a happy New Year. The last TV act of the evening was finishing her song, and the audience was asked to come to the floor and join the dance under the giant disco ball. Chetan and his brother were dancing along, trying to copy the moves from the TV and borrowing some from Mithun Chakraborty, the dance phenomenon. The TV volume remained low. Chetan could barely hear the song or the dancing from the kitchen. The countdown began, and the

21

family counted along with the TV anchor.

Eight, seven, six, five, four, three, two, one . . .

"Happy New Year!" The kids hugged Mom and Dad, but Mom and Dad did not hug each other. They did not indulge in public displays of affection, even at home.

Rat-a-tat-tat. Rat-a-tat-tat. Sudden menacing popping and booming put an immediate stop to the celebrations. These could not be firecrackers, although it would not be uncommon to welcome the New Year with blazing fireworks for the rest of the country. But not there in Patiala, not in Punjab. In those days, it could mean only one thing. An automatic weapon. An AK-47. The noise appeared to come from someplace far away. It did not seem to be from the neighborhood.

"Sounds like a gunfire," exclaimed startled Vijay.

Everyone came into motion as if they'd rehearsed the maneuver several times. Chetan and Vikki instinctively ducked and got closer to the floor. Chetan's mother ran to the kitchen to turn the solitary light that was still on. Dad held the field hockey stick in his hand as he turned off the TV. Mom carefully stepped back into the room with a lighted candle in her hand, and the kids were hiding on the side of the bed opposite the door that faced the front of the house.

A few police sirens broke the silence, which gave Chetan and his family little to no relief. It was hard to determine if the police were real or if someone was impersonating them. Distrust was at an all-time high. The rule was not to open the door, no matter who it was, especially not at night.

Chetan and Vikki were indoctrinated to mistrust everyone. Iron grills protected the glass windows of their home, and doors were double-bolted from the inside. The main gate, a mere four feet high, was secured by a padlock. It was not a significant deterrent if someone really wanted to barge in. There was a commotion outside the house, and Vijay moved the window curtains slightly to peek outside.

" It's the neighbors talking to our chowkidar," he said softly.

"What's he saying?" Renu whispered from a distance.

"Looks like there was no one on our street."

The chowkidar, an aging security guard of the neighborhood, was waving people off, indicating that he did not see anyone passing through the lane. Even if he did see anything, he was not bold enough to admit it. He was there just to do his job of deterring petty theft and carjackings and to make ends meet. He would not try to be a hero and risk his life. He would never admit to seeing anything or anyone, lest police take him for questioning for the next several days.

People feared police interrogation. It was mostly done un-documented. There would be no proof that they apprehended a person, what they did to the person, and where they dumped the person once they were done with their interrogation. Police would not write a formal report, and there was no reading of your rights or access to a lawyer. There was no notion of fundamental rights in those times. It all seemed like a scene from an apocalyptic movie, where anarchy and purging had taken over the cities, and the only way to get through was to fight or hide till all was over.

Within a few minutes, the noises were subdued, and the street was again engulfed in silent darkness, pierced by the intermittent whistle of the chowkidar.

Suddenly, the phone rang, and Chetan's mother picked it up. Another thing Chetan's family learned during that period was to have the female in the household pick up the phone, especially late at night. If an unknown person asked about

23

Vijay's whereabouts, she would say he was out of town and hang up. The logic was that the insurgents would come after adult males—females and kids were usually spared.

"Hello," she answered.

"Hello, are you all okay?" It was Mrs. Randhawa on the other side.

"Yes, we are fine." She was so relieved to hear the landlady's voice that tears fell from her eyes.

"Good. But if you want, you can come upstairs and spend the night here."

"Thank you, Mrs. Randhawa. Do not worry, we'll be fine."

"Okay, but let us know if you need anything. And yes, happy New Year."

"Happy New Year."

Chetan studied his mother's face. White with fear, eyes wet despite her attempts to wipe the tears off so the kids could not see them. She was a brave woman, the rock of the family. Usually, nothing would unnerve her easily, but these were not usual times. The coarse winds of time eroded the family rock one grain at a time. The firing of guns was not an isolated incident. Killings were recurring day after day with ever-increasing brutality. It was becoming unbearable to live under constant fear, and she would often plead to Vijay to move to Delhi. The jobs were not easy to come by, and he had just gotten a promotion. The move would have to wait for the right time and opportunity. For now, it was all about keeping one's head down and surviving the storm.

"Let's all go to bed," she said.

Chetan and his brother went to their rooms. Chetan's room was next to his parents. He could not sleep. He could hear his mother crying. Chetan wanted to walk up to her and say

24

something but could not gather enough courage. He did not know what to say to her. She was the strongest person he knew, and hearing her cry made Chetan miserable. Laying on his bed, Chetan stared at the ceiling fan and prayed with his hands folded under his comforter. He continued to pray and hoped for better days as they ushered in the new year.

And, thus, it began: the year 1984.

3

Renu Malhotra

The year 1984 had arrived—the year that George Orwell made famous. Was there any truth to Orwell's prognostication? How relevant that would be to Punjab, India. No doubt, there were signs of totalitarianism and oppressive regimes. There was surveillance, fundamental rights were suspended, and the press was not free. It was hard to discern truth from lies and policies from political agendas, and citizens were constantly manipulated for someone's gain.

Emotions ran high, and any spark of confrontation would set the community ablaze. The public had no faith in the police as protectors—they operated more like predators. The government's actions, including curfews, media censorship, and extrajudicial killings, created an atmosphere of fear and suspicion reminiscent of Orwell's Oceania. Even innocent people would change their path if they saw the police coming from the other side. Police were to be avoided at any cost. If you carefully looked, examples of doublethink and thoughtcrime could be found around you.

Even Orwell could not have imagined what would happen in Punjab that year. The events in Punjab were a harrowing reality for countless individuals who suffered under the political chaos. For the people of Punjab, there would be no freedom from the shackles of mind control, as illustrated so dramatically by Apple's iconic Super Bowl commercial, in which they'd introduce Macintosh to the world this very month. Macintosh was not going to emancipate the people of Punjab from their suffering this year. Sometimes, as they say, truth is stranger than fiction.

Renu had never heard of George Orwell or his novel *1984*. She had never heard about Macintosh either. She was born into a farming family, although a wealthy one. She was abundantly provided for and received a good education, considering she was a girl child and from a wealthy farming family. They lived in a large bungalow near their farmland in the city of Ferozepur, Punjab. She graduated with a bachelor's degree in music. Chetan was bewildered when she first told him she had a music degree. Although she was very fond of Hindi film music and her day started with turning up the radio to listen to *Vividh Bharti* for the latest songs, she had not played any instrument since her marriage to Vijay.

"I played sitar in college," she would say.

Chetan found it amusing. "You are joking. I do not believe you."

"I have a college degree in music to prove it," Renu insisted.

She even showed Chetan her sitar once on their visit to her parents' home. Her day was spent on household chores. Preparing meals, supervising the servants that would come to sweep the house, wash dishes, and do the laundry. She had also taken it upon herself to be the primary caretaker of the

27

kids and their studies. She was good at keeping track of each homework assignment and test. During the exam days, she spent hours at length preparing sample tests for Chetan and Vikki, made them memorize the answers, and had them recite those back to her. She was fully invested in their education.

Renu had a privileged childhood. She was the eldest of three siblings. She, her younger sister, and her brother grew up with half a dozen servants to serve in their household, 24/7. She was the most pampered one. Her very fair skin, silky brown hair, and almost emerald-green eyes prompted people to call her *Angrez*, the term used for a British person. The lighter skin made you superior. With a regal aura surrounding her, Renu carried herself with the poise of a princess. She was confident and strong and never was the one to back away from a fight. There was no particular pressure of education on her as it was assumed that she would not have to work to earn a living and would be married off when the time came.

Before her marriage to Vijay, her time was spent fooling around the town with her girlfriends, watching movies at the local cinema, and eating out. The family went out regularly for picnics at their farm, where Renu wandered through the fields of swaying wheat and the fragrant citrus orchards that colored the landscape. She was most peaceful there. Although, her favorite palace to visit was the city of Ludhiana, where she had her uncles and aunts. Ludhiana was a much larger city than her hometown, Ferozepur. The shopping scene was so much better in Ludhiana; moreover, her uncles living there owned a couple of restaurants and a movie theater. What's not to love? She would always find a reason to escape to Ludhiana. She grew up almost shuttling between the two cities, and when it was time for her wedding, of course, the city of choice for her was Ludhiana.

Renu expected married life to be a bed of roses, full of picnics, shopping, and travel. She pleaded with her mother to marry her into a business family. Renu wanted to continue her rich lifestyle, with enough money, resources, and freedom to enjoy her life. Her mother, on the other hand, did not find the business owners or farming people very sophisticated and preferred a groom who was well-educated and a professional working in the corporate world. Renu's mom won, and the clash of worlds happened. Renu's mother agreed to a match who was an engineer by education but had no more than a penny to his name. Her mother was convinced that, because of the good education, he would be successful and her daughter Renu would be better off moving away from the life of farming landlords.

After she wedded Vijay Malhotra, who worked at a well-reputed corporation, Renu moved from her seven-bedroom bungalow to a two-bedroom rental unit in Patiala. There, she lived with her husband and her mother-in-law. They had no servants, no cooks, and no cleaners. Her dreams came shattering down. Her mother-in-law's constant bickering and condemnation about her incompetence in managing the household chores and her inability to cook added to the agony.

"All you know is fashion. A simple dal you cannot make," Renu's mother-in-law would taunt.

"Well, I never had to. We had servants doing that," Renu would retort. And, the fight would start.

"Did no one teach you the manners to talk to elders?"

"If you do not like the sabzi I make, ask your son to hire a cook!"

"We do not eat food made by the hands of cooks!"

"Why? You do not have any issues eating samosas from the bazaar! Who do you think cooks those?" To add to Renu's despair, the Malhotra family was vegetarian, and she loved chicken curry.

The fights were constant and would invariably end in both of them crying and lamenting about their fate. Vijay was busy with his office work, and Renu was left alone at home to deal with her mother-in-law. No one had equipped Renu to handle such a situation. In those days, they had no phone, so the only way to communicate with her parents was via postal letters. She was lonely, unsupported, and frustrated. When Vijay returned from the office, both Renu and Vijay's mother would compete for his attention, and there were complaints from both sides. Vijay would do little to placate matters or resolve any altercation. He was too timid to face his wife or to confront his mother. Renu got increasingly frustrated with his attitude of avoiding confrontation at all costs, which made matters worse, both for Renu and for her mother-in-law. He would keep listening to the grumblings from both sides. He was called mother's pony, wife's slave, henpecked husband, and unfair and unjust husband, and he would just listen. He would not respond, and that made Renu absolutely livid.

"At least say something! Why don't you ever have anything to say?"

"What do you want me to say?" he'd respond, hiding behind his newspaper. That newspaper became a barrier between them, and he would often hide behind it. Any confrontation would result in raising the newspaper and a signal to Renu that all her pleas would fall on deaf ears.

During these times of despair and desolation, Chetan was born in 1973, just fifteen months after the marriage. He was not the cutest newborn. He was dark, almost bluish-black, due to the trauma of a difficult delivery and low oxygen levels. His head had violent marks of the forceps that doctors had to use to pull him out, as if he did not want to be born. Renu's first reaction to seeing her firstborn was not love, adulation, or completeness; it was disgust and repulsion. The mother-in-law did not miss this opportunity to taunt her.

"This is what you deserve for being disrespectful," she said. "I got scared when I saw your child," she added.

"Why? Did you not get scared when your son was born?" Renu would not take things lying down.

Renu was almost ashamed to show her newborn to anyone. Not only did she have to deal with an ugly creature, but a newborn added to an already insurmountable workload. Her dreams of the independence, travel, and enjoyment associated with the marriage, all came shattering down. Meanwhile, among all the chaos, Chetan was growing and gaining strength in spite of the first signs of being the unwelcome one.

However, things did change for the better. The constant fighting was too much for the aging mother-in-law to handle, and in a couple of years, she moved out to live with Vijay's elder brother. Vijay was growing in his career, and so was his paycheck. He started spending a lot more time at his office. Chetan, too, shed his blue birthmarks and became a more socially acceptable color—wheatish. He gained weight and turned into an adorable, chubby toddler. The family began to reach a level of normalcy and compromise, but Renu and Chetan continued to have a love-hate relationship. There were times of affection, but Chetan would often be an easy target for her jeering and at the receiving end of her frustrations. At times, his mischief and antics would make Renu laugh; at other times, it would mean an angry slap across his face.

The year 1984 would stress test the family even more. The Malhotras would be pushed to the brink to test their faith, commitment, and togetherness. Renu had not visited her parents in eight months, which was unusual for her, as she normally would visit them about every three months. An escape from the daily drudgery of household chores. Her sanctum solarium. But travel was dangerous, especially to her parents' place in Ferozepur, near the Pakistan border— the hotbed of commotion, religious clashes, and violence instigated by insurgents.

The last time Renu and the kids traveled to Ferozepur, it was a stressful bus trip. Renu prepared the two boys in case their bus came under attack. The bus had to navigate through the areas with the most unrest, and killings of people traveling by bus were not uncommon. There were frequent reports of armed men stopping the buses, pulling Hindu men out, and shooting them. Children needed to be well-prepared for the journey. If they were to face any such situation, they would pose to be Sikhs. Renu gave them pretend Sikh names—Kartar and Angad— and she would be Amarjeet. Both kids wore *kada*, a heavy steel bracelet on their right hand, a symbol of Sikhism.

"Why do you say your hair is cut?" she rehearsed with kids at home. Sikh boys kept long hair tied in a bun on top of the head covered with a *patka*, a larger-sized handkerchief, to cover their heads till they were old enough to wear a turban. Renu needed an excuse for why her sons had their hair cut.

"We came from Delhi, and there we had to cut our hair for safety," Chetan regurgitated.

That visit was last April, after the kids had completed their final exams.

Being locked up in the house took its toll on Renu. The kids had an outlet in the form of their school, and Vijay had his office to go to. She was stuck at home, and her social interactions were limited to the other ladies in the neighborhood. The more she thought about it, the worse she felt. The feeling of being trapped at home got worse with every passing day. She missed going out for a movie, shopping with friends, eating out, and visiting her parents. The daily rut of cooking, getting the kids ready for school, cleaning, and cooking some more became increasingly burdensome.

Moreover, the daily news of killings, kidnappings, bus hijackings, and bomb blasts was not something anyone could get used to. The incidents kept occurring, and they were now seeping into the inner layers of society and neighborhoods. People were increasingly getting suspicious of each other. Men who lived like brothers for decades and celebrated Diwali and Gurpurab together were now avoiding each other. There was an awkwardness about addressing each other with either namaste or with *Sat Sri Akaal*. There was too much pride and hatred to use the other religion's greetings. Unlike Vijay, Renu was not very religious. She did not pray every day as Vijay did and had no qualms about eating eggs on Tuesdays, which was a big no for any observing Hindu family, even if they were non-vegetarians. But in those days, people were becoming less tolerant of other religions and wearing their religious passions on their sleeves.

More than anything, Renu feared that they would be subjected to a social boycott by others in the Hindu community if they were seen not following required Hindu rituals or if they were seen as overly compassionate toward the Sikh community.

Irritation, mistrust, and general discontent among people led to frequent clashes. Intolerance was at an all-time high. The economy was suffering, and unemployment was rampant. The youth had nothing better to do than to loiter on the street. They would find pride in claiming an association with some popular Hindu or Sikh religious faction, even if it was untrue. Unoccupied youth would routinely carry out small-time robberies and make threatening calls, asking for ransom, using the names of these factions.

Renu was worried. She was living in a house owned by Sikhs. It was a two-edged sword. On one side, she felt safer, but on the other hand, she could be facing the wrath of other Hindus. What if one day, the homeowner were to throw their family out? If it happened during the riots, it would mean a certain death. During one of her afternoon knitting sessions with Mrs. Randhawa, it eventually came up.

"Police are getting totally out of control and unfairly troubling Sikh families. This is the land of Sikhs, and they need to respect that," said Mrs. Randhawa.

Land of Sikhs? This is the land of the earliest civilizations, the land that has been inhabited for four thousand years, Renu thought.

"So, are you going to throw us out?" she asked, her eyes locked into Mrs. Randhawa's eyes. They stared at each other, unblinking.

"Of course not! You are in our protection. Sikhs never betray those who come under their protection. That's what the gurus have taught us."

Renu smiled. *The protection.* An air of pride swirled around

Mrs. Randhawa, but she meant every word she said. They would give their lives to shield the Malhotras. But what about the other Sikh neighbors? Would they be as tolerant and protective of Renu and her family if the unthinkable happened?

Renu's daily routine began with sending the kids and husband off. She then continued pacing the house anxiously until they returned. Evenings could become even more strained. After a day full of stress, Renu and Vijay would be packed to the brim like a pressure cooker, and the cooker would explode once in a while. Their fights were ugly. The children would go to their rooms and hide. Most fights ended with Renu crying and Vijay skipping dinner and going straight to bed. There was no attempt to resolve the situation or to sit down and discuss why they both were so stressed out. Renu and Vijay lacked those communication skills.

The aftermath of their fights was never good for Chetan. In her anger and frustration, Renu invariably lashed at him. The slightest provocation by Chetan would result in a severe beating for him. There were days when the pain from the beatings was so severe that he could not sleep. Renu could hear him sobbing under the blanket, but she was too angry to pacify him.

Renu once confessed to her sister that Chetan had received an unfair share of beatings from her, that she could not control herself, and, in her frustration, lashed out at him. Chetan was listening, feeling good, knowing it was not his fault. Anytime Renu would say a word of praise for him or when she talked to her friends about his school report with pride, he would be over the moon.

All was not lost between them.

Chetan was too young to understand where the sudden burst of Mom's anger came from. He did not understand that his mother had not yet reconciled to marrying a man with limited resources. He did not understand that his mother's dreams were squashed. She had to learn a totally new way of life, a life that had become an everyday struggle of lack of money, hard work, and minimal social status. All that Renu had taken for granted before her marriage was now hard to come by. Chetan grew up feeling unloved, feeling like a burden. He kept his fears, doubts, and needs to himself to avoid adding more to Renu's misery. He was often confused and uncertain, looked for belonging, and tried to figure out how he might be at fault and how he had deserved such a lack of affection from his mother.

The boy wondered why his father remained a silent observer, as if the matter of Chetan's misery did not concern him. Why did he never rescue him from Renu's wrath? His father was right there, witnessing the abuse, but he did not try to put a stop to it. Was his father so devoid of love that he could not see his pain, or did he think that Renu had the full right to do whatever was needed to keep the boys in line? Was Vijay's only responsibility to put the food on the table, and then he was done?

Looking toward his father for his rescue was futile; Chetan realized that early on. Vijay remained aloof, as he had no courage to intervene and had too big an ego to admit it. It was the same trait that had earlier prevented Vijay from mediating between his mother and his wife, and now it kept him from rescuing his son. Chetan did not want to be like his father—a coward.

Chetan wanted to win Renu's love, her affection, her admiration, something that he had craved since he was a baby. Despite often being subjected to her anger and ridicule, Chetan had an unwavering respect and love for his mother. The more Renu denied him her affection, the harder he tried to win her over. Whenever he aced a school exam, Chetan proudly ran to his mother and showed his work. Every painting he produced, every craft he created—all were attempts to win his mother's adoration. Times were not making it easy for him, but he was not the one to give up on her.

Renu's approval and her validation became core to Chetan's existence. He learned avoidance as his way of survival: keep quiet, lie low, do not speak up, and never question. He was conditioned to be cautious, always on edge, and not to believe in any idea of happily ever after. For him, happiness was always short-lived and made him think because he was happy, there must be some indignity and suffering lurking in the corner. He habituated to embracing pain more easily; the pain had some notion of finality to it, and happiness was so transient. He always expected failure; the worst outcomes awaited every idea, thought, or proposal. He became his devil's advocate, talked himself out of any happiness, and sabotaged any faintest possibility of joy.

4

February 1984: The Lull Before the Storm

Chetan sat wide-eyed before the television, captivated by breaking news. The space shuttle *Challenger* had embarked on a historic mission—an untethered spacewalk. Without any lifeline, the two astronauts put their fate into the hands of tiny jets to explore the dark—a spectacle of the human quest for knowledge and conquering new frontiers. Chetan collected newspaper clippings, sketched astronauts in his drawing book, and dreamt of a future where he, too, could travel and explore new places. The *Challenger* mission was an impressive feat of courage and ingenuity, as humans let go of straps, free from the pull of gravity, and floated in space as satellites.

Down on earth, in the state of Punjab, in sharp contrast, people were getting increasingly tangled in the web of religion, politics, and power. As the world was reaching new heights, Punjab was sinking deeper into the quicksand of lawlessness and violence. Every action and every movement made to get out of the quicksand pulled its people an inch farther in.

The situation was getting dirtier and bloodier and reaching a point where the options to regain any normalcy were severely limited.

February began with a call for a daylong strike to support the resolution for regional autonomy for the state of Punjab. It was a carefully orchestrated and well-publicized event, and every city, including Chetan's hometown of Patiala, was expected to comply. The insurgents were the enforcers of the lockdown. They came with their sticks, rods, and swords and made rounds across the city to ensure the public complied with the full closure. Any shop, store, or even a pharmacy they found open was forced to shut down. Street vendors selling vegetables door-to-door were beaten up and sent back to their homes. The only places left open were a few *dhabas*—roadside restaurants—and medical shops on the sides of the Rajendra Hospital main entrance, on "humanitarian grounds."

Some strike organizers stood at the gates of neighborhoods, monitoring people's every movement. Any car or scooter seen on the road was asked to turn back, first nicely, and if they resisted, then strikers pulled out iron rods. Vehicles with press decals were allowed to pass. The media coverage was necessary, and inviting the press to verify the strike's success was important. Other vehicles that could pass were ones with the Red Cross logo painted on them, deemed driven by a doctor or other medical professional. All doctors would put a Red Cross sign on their vehicles, though it never meant they actually belonged to the Red Cross. Doctors were permitted, as no group wanted a poor reputation for denying treatment to the sick. The insurgents wanted to leverage every emotion to gain support for their cause—using strength, showing compassion, gaining sympathy, and, when needed, instilling fear.

Sporadic incidents of violence across the state marked the day. Newspapers noted that fifteen people had been injured in various clashes between Hindus and Sikhs. Police were tightening their stronghold and rounding up people in jails. More than a hundred people were arrested across the state for charges ranging from disrupting road traffic to throwing stones at shops and thrashing people who dared to open their businesses during the strike.

Chetan's family knew that one simply followed the orders on such days. Some faction or other would call a strike, and city closure would happen. This meant closing all businesses, shops, colleges, and schools. And sometimes, the police and administration ordered a curfew, and everything came to a standstill. In any case, it meant people should stay home and lie low. Vijay always ensured that they had enough rations for a couple of weeks in case things shut down for an extended period. People were already feeling the shortage of vegetables, eggs, and bread. They would store staples like wheat, rice, onions, potatoes, oil, and a few kinds of dals. During those times, it was good to know someone serving in the army. That connection could help a person move around the city in the government-provided Jonga, get a shop open, or obtain some rations from the military canteen when in dire need. There were never any attacks on the army vehicles in the city. Truth be told, Chetan and Vikki would love the strikes since that meant a day off from school, and if the strike fell on an exam day, that was a reason for celebration.

Chetan was in sixth grade, and Vikki in fourth. Exam days were upon them, and the two boys would be heads down studying; Chetan constantly battled high anxiety during exam times. He had to work hard for grades, and the consequences of not getting good grades were severe. The more stressed he got about the exams, the more mistakes he would make. Mistakes like accidentally skipping a few questions or not calculating sums correctly were what teachers would call "silly mistakes." His mother would not forgive such silly mistakes, and it would call for severe punishment.

Chetan's mother was, as usual, prepping them for the school exams, creating the practice tests, doing the chapter reviews, and checking their work. Chetan spent the day memorizing chapters and writing the practice tests Mom prepared. She only permitted him a break for lunch. He did not go out for any play and kept reading until late in the evening. Time after dinner was meant for the final review and checks. Vikki had already completed all his preparations and revisions and sat relaxed. Vikki was excellent in his studies and could easily cruise through the exams. A trait that Chetan lacked. For Chetan, the process was quite laborious. He had to read chapters multiple times, recite them loudly a few times, and write everything down before he got ready. Renu sat on the bed next to Chetan and started asking him questions from the syllabus. Chetan was reciting the answers back, sometimes closing his eyes to help him recollect. His hands were clasped tight in front of him, and he rocked back and forth as he answered. He sat at a distance that Renu's hand could not reach—just in case he forgot an answer.

There were rumors that exams could be postponed, although that was not something Chetan wanted to happen. He wanted to be done with the pressures of exams and enjoy the spring break stress-free. The anticipation of upcoming exams was too unnerving, and the fear of the impending riots added to

41

his anxiety. Every year, after the exams, they would go to their grandparents' palace in Ferozepur, a break they really looked forward to. Chetan found his mother to be the happiest at his grandparents' home. Great food, including chicken and mutton curry, and several servants at their disposal who would cook whatever she demanded and take the kids out to play whenever they wanted. The trip would not be possible this year, although Chetan hoped they all could get a break.

The ongoing political clashes confused Chetan. It seemed more complex than just a Hindu-Sikh clash. Chetan was too young to grasp the intricate politics of circumstances when the skirmishes happened within the same religious groups. For him, everyone was surrounded by a constant lingering fear that was routinely reinforced by bloodshed. Politicians were making their moves to grab as much power as they could. The worst crisis brought an enormous opportunity, and leaders were conniving to influence the power centers and control the narrative to their advantage. There were clashes among various Sikh groups amid the ongoing struggle to gain control of the narrative. Any leadership on the rise was accused of being power-hungry, and any attempts at peace talks were labeled as selling off the soul to the devil—the central government.

Many new leaders emerged, many vanished, and many were killed on both the Hindu and Sikh sides. Still, new leaders kept sprouting. Such was the allure of power, position, and a big payoff for the last person standing. For Chetan, it all seemed to be a never-ending, scary nightmare. Living in constant fear and being cautious of every step and every movement was robbing him and thousands of kids of a normal childhood. Fear of school, fear of riots, and fear of his mother became

42

his constant companion. He found himself always walking on eggshells, ever so carefully. He could not do much about the riots, but every night, he prayed for a better day in school, to get good grades, and somehow to deserve his mother's love.

Chetan's father came home from his office on time, and Chetan followed his daily routine. He rushed outside and opened the gates of the house to let his car in. Once Dad was on his chair and had removed his shoes and socks, Chetan fetched him a glass of water, took his shoes away, put them in the closet, and grabbed evening slippers, *chappals*, and the newspaper for his father, who would put the TV on. The news began with an incident involving an attack on a wedding procession—crude bombs injured six people, but no deaths were reported. Chetan stood next to his father's chair, eyes locked on the TV. Mom had knitting needles in her hand, finishing the last remaining sweater she had planned for the season.

"Why would you plan wedding processions these days?" Vijay remarked. "Is the show-off really necessary in such times? They can do a court marriage,"

"Sure, you don't have fun, nor should anyone else," Mom retorted immediately, as if waiting to find an opening to complain. "It has been two weeks since I stepped outside the house. I would rather die outside than rot in here." Her frustration was evident from her pale, tired face.

Chetan could tell things had neared the boiling point. He took a few steps back. Dad merely raised his newspaper, the barrier between him and Mom. She knitted faster, more furiously. Chetan backed farther away, out of their bedroom.

The tension had not eased at the dinner table. Chetan kept his head down and ate fast. Renu and Vijay's twelfth wedding

43

anniversary was approaching in a few days, further straining the atmosphere.

Vijay looked at Renu. "How about we go out for a movie?"

"What? Which one?" A sudden excitement exuded from Renu.

"I heard good things about *Tohfa*," Vijay proposed.

"Wow! So, you are keeping track of movies these days." There was a note of sarcasm in Renu's voice.

The new superhit musical *Tohfa*, starring Jeetendra and Jaya Prada, took over India and was number one on the box office list. It was released at the same time as *Footloose*, but Jeetendra's powerful hip gyrations made Kevin Bacon's dance moves seem muted.

Going to the movie theater was not without danger. Most families had stopped going out to watch movies, and theaters were mostly visited by college students, single men, or laborers who would find a reprieve in the theater after the day's hard work. Even though people were strongly discouraged from going to the cinema, there have been no recent incidents in Patiala. Renu happily agreed, and Chetan took a deep sigh of relief.

On the day of the movie, Vijay and Renu left Chetan and Vikki under the supervision of Mrs. Randhawa, who would make phone calls several times to check up on them. Chetan was instructed not to open the door for anyone, to keep the noise down, and to finish his homework. Chetan followed the instructions to a T, except for the study part. Chetan remained restless and got up every few minutes to check if the doors were bolted properly and if the windows were shut. His caution was becoming compulsive. Chetan put on the TV to alleviate his anxiety but was unable to sit through the entire

44

TV program.

Delhi Doordarshan, the national TV channel, was broadcast-ing the recording of the Grammy Awards. The King of Pop had just taken over the TV—Michael Jackson. *Thriller* was all the rage, even in the riot-struck Punjab. Chetan watched MJ take away his record eight Grammys, yet Chetan's mind constantly wondered. At every commercial break or in response to any noise, he went around the house checking the locks, unlocking and relocking them repeatedly. He was the elder one and tried to stay strong in front of his brother, but inside, he just wanted to scream and hide. Vikki was at ease, watching TV, but Chetan remained anxious, making rounds of the house. He tried to distract himself by thinking about a new poster for his room—which had to be MJ.

In the heart of Patiala, where Chetan's neighborhood once echoed with laughter and cricket games, things began to change. Suddenly, the peaceful streets became riddled with lawlessness – breaking into houses, stealing, and even beating people on the road. Police said it was routine, but it felt anything but ordinary. The adults spoke in hushed tones, and the stories of violence filled the radio news. It was like a dark cloud had settled over, and Chetan couldn't escape its shadow.

Clashes started to spread to nearby states like Haryana, Himachal, and Rajasthan as well. It was mid-February when the trouble reached Haryana, and Chetan couldn't escape the news that more than twelve people lost their lives there. It was all over the TV. The air felt heavy with anger and hatred, spread like wildfire that nobody could control.

The world outside was noticing, too. Newspapers like the New York Times covered what was happening in Punjab as much as the local ones like the Tribune, the Times of India, or the Punjab Kesari. Every day, it seemed like the fights were getting worse, with more people getting hurt and losing their lives. Streets once used for playing cricket became battlefields, with young men fighting with sticks, rods, and swords. It was like a dangerous game, and Chetan didn't understand why they were doing it.

This strange power struggle was like a game to own the streets. It wasn't about protests anymore but about fear and anger turning into something else. At times, Chetan would encounter young men charging into the streets with weapons, fueled by fiery animosity and manic hatred. Those were the scariest moments for him. Chetan watched gangs injure each other with steel rods and cricket bats, and it didn't make any sense. They enjoyed it like a game to see who could hurt the most. It made Chetan sick to his stomach.

One afternoon, as Chetan rode his bicycle home from school, a Hindu group of two dozen or so were marching across the bazaar in Patiala, brandishing their tridents and rods and forcing the shopkeepers to shut down, the ones who were daring enough to keep their shops open still. The vegetable shop owner, who had his shop still open, tried to resist the raging protesters. He was forcibly dragged out of his shop and beaten mercilessly. Chetan looked away, thinking about his own beatings at home. He wondered if it would hurt for days as it did for him. He was scared and felt sorry for the shopkeeper. He felt helpless, knowing he could not save him. He knew him. He and his father visited that shop frequently. Every time Chetan was there, the owner would give Chetan an apple or an orange for free. Chetan loved his warm smile.

But today, Chetan could not make eye contact with him. The owner cried out loud as his beating continued, but Chetan looked away. He wondered if he would ever have the courage to step in and save someone in a similar situation.

The lockdown proceeded with success, and all small shops, businesses, and schools were closed, but Vijay had to go to the office. His office operated 24/7 and never shut down for the strikes. The company would get the exemption from the administration as well as immunity from all the local leaders and groups by donating to their causes. The cost of doing business.

Renu was extra nervous for Vijay during the days of protests and lockdowns, but he did not have a stay-at-home option. Any day Vijay took longer than expected to return home, there was a palpable tension in the house. Renu would pace outside along the driveway, and Chetan would curl up in the corner of his room, trying to distract himself by painting landscapes, his favorite hobby. Still, it was never enough to overcome the fear.

Chetan was a natural at painting. He had books full of his watercolor landscapes and portraits. Bottled Camel watercolors and a set of paintbrushes were among his prized possessions. He was incredibly proud of the portrait he painted of the first Sikh guru, Guru Nanak Dev. The painting got a lot of praise from his schoolteacher, who recommended that Chetan get that painting framed against a black background. His painting of Guru Nanak Dev, adorned in saffron garb, closed eyes, folded hands, and deep in meditation, brought peace to Chetan. But the painting was never framed. Vijay had brushed the idea off.

On such stressful days, Chetan painted more and prayed harder. He clasped the *om* pendant that he had purchased from the street vendors sitting in front of Kali Mandir and continued praying for his dad's safe return. His other hand grabbed the steel kada bracelet on his wrist.

Let Dad be safe; let him come home, he kept repeating in his head until his Dad finally entered the house.

The habit had become compulsive.

Ten-year-old Chetan had pictures and small statues of various gods—Krishna, Ram, Kali Devi, and Ganesha—in his room, juxtaposing the Elton John and Lendl posters. Among other pictures were Bhagat Singh and Chandrashekhar Azaad, the two brave freedom fighters who gave the ultimate sacrifice for the country. One Sikh and the other Hindu. Chetan wanted to be brave like them and wanted to harness the power of Kali, but bravery did not come naturally to him.

The violence continued, and the death count for the past two weeks shot up to sixty-eight, per the official report. Actual numbers were expected to be much higher. As the incidents grew, Gurdwara Sri Harmandir Sahib, the Golden Temple, became the center of control. The abode of God, the Darbar Sahib, the most significant shrine in Sikhism, the one that was repeatedly destroyed by the Mughal and rose time and again, became the focal point once again.

No one expected what was going to happen in the next few months. Extraordinary escalations would change the history of Punjab and India forever. The situation was past any peaceful resolution, and no one wanted to concede an inch. The violence was not giving peace any chance, and no talks could be fruitful in such circumstances.

Chetan's fears took deeper roots. Intermittent days of anxiousness turned into thick layers of anxiety, gloom, dread, and panic that started to settle on his psyche. No matter how hard he tried, he could not break through those. A continuous sense of doom overtook him. Something terrible was going to happen happen. The dread stole his dreams, desires, and hope. Any sign of happiness was just a forewarning of a disaster about to happen.

5

March 1984: The Unrest

It was March 1984, and the Cold War would continue for another seven years until the dissolution of the Soviet Union. There were no direct conflicts between the United States and the USSR, but that did not mean that both were not always plotting their next move for world domination and control by supporting and promoting proxy wars across the globe.

The unrest in India presented another opportunity for the two world leaders to demonstrate their strength and increase their influence in the Indian subcontinent. Everyone wanted their share of the pie, and unrest in this part of the world smelled like an opportunity to so many. Nations, defense contractors, arms manufacturers, and infrastructure developers were salivating at the prospect of getting their share. Any unrest and dozens of stakeholders emerge—countries like the United States, USSR, Canada, the UK, Pakistan, China, Bangladesh—political parties across the globe. Unions of farmers, laborers, students, nonprofit organizations, and intelligence administrations such as the KGB, the CIA,

ISI, and RAW—all were looking for an opportunity to use the situation to their benefit, to increase their power and influence.

No one really thinks about the ordinary people, like Chetan and his family, who were suffering every day because of the ulterior motives of so many. Who was the director and producer of this play that they all unwillingly became a part of? Who could people go to and plead for mercy? Who should they blame? Who to go to for safety and protection? The puppet master hid himself well.

Everyone seemed to be a vulture in this decaying jungle, waiting for another body to fall. All of them proclaimed and preached about a bigger cause they were fighting for, and proclaimed that the death and carnage were merely unavoidable collateral damage. The reasons were beyond the conception of ordinary men because the violence was justified by ideologies that contradicted the principles of faith. Rules, principles, and laws were never so disconnected.

Somehow, Chetan, his family, and millions of others were supposed to pass through this inferno, prove their affiliations, their integrity, their loyalties to the country, to the society, to their religion, and try to survive, hoping things would be better once a resolution was reached. But for the resolution, they all had to pass through this wildfire that would take the form of the devil itself and devour thousands before showing any signs of slowing down.

Chetan could hear that devil's breath every time he stepped out, every time it was dark outside, and every time he was alone. Every night, the devil would come out, and the faded red nightlight of his bedroom did little to keep the devil away. The guttural and deep sound emitted such heat that it could melt skin, and its odor would make one nauseated. But it did not kill; Chetan had to bear it and tolerate it. As the devil wrapped itself around Chetan, he would want to scream, and he would want to cry, but no sound would come from his mouth. Finding himself in the burning heat, all Chetan could do was keep staring at the wall with the pictures of gods, curled in his bed, waiting to fall asleep. Occasionally, a mirage of hope would manifest before him, the appearance of a god fighting the devil to the ground and saving him for that day. This devil tormented Chetan daily, and the darkness was seeping within him and eating him from the inside out. The smell of this boiling poison remained with him forever, burning holes in his soul that would take years to shrink. The sheer sense of helplessness, the feeling of being a puppet with a complete lack of control, and the loneliness amid the chaos defined Chetan's 1984.

Discussions about local and international politics were routine. Whenever a visitor came home, Chetan heard discussions evolving into debates about the USSR, India, Pakistan, and the USA. Despite the complex international politics, in Chetan's simplistic mind, the USSR supported India, and the USA protected and assisted Pakistan. Therefore, any incident between the USA and the USSR represented who had the edge, India or Pakistan.

Sitting in front of the TV and listening to the news about US and USSR military misadventures would raise many questions in Chetan's head.

Will the Soviet Union help us if Pakistan attacks India?

Is the US aiding Pakistan to destroy India? Why is the US so against India?

Will China attack India again?

Such questions agitated Chetan, and they would send him

spiraling down the path of one lousy thought after another, and his imagination always ended up with some worst-case scenario. Any TV news of tension at the border of India and Pakistan or India and China would push him into endless analysis. Curled up in his bed, he brooded over possible air strikes. He tried to plan out how he would get out of the city. He tried to recite his grandparents' and uncle's phone numbers. He tried to visualize what buses he would take if he and Vikki needed to escape from Patiala. The constant anxiety was something he could not shrug off, and the fear of doomsday, in which his family would be destroyed in some bloody war, never gave him a moment's peace. He could not shirk these thoughts; any grim news or rumor would trigger panic.

With the rise of American influence worldwide, Chetan was clear that it was with the US that India should align.

The US is so strong and mighty. If we were friends with the US, India would be different.

How does India benefit from its alliance with the Soviet Union anyway?

Although, for Chetan, the India-USSR friendship had some free goodies in it for him as a consolation. The Soviet Union and its Mir Publishers would send free books and comics to India. His mom had subscribed to children's magazines from the Soviet Union, which arrived monthly through the Indian postal service. Occasionally, Mir Publishers' bookstore-on-the-bus would come to Chetan's school, donate books to the library, and sell books to students at throwaway prices.

Chetan loved their books on physics and chemistry. He would also search for short stories by Tolstoy and books teaching how to draw and paint. Chetan was obsessed with the pencil sketches in those books, especially the one of Leo Tolstoy himself. He would copy that sketch onto his drawing book again and again. He did that so often that he could draw Tolstoy from his memory. The quality of the books, with their glossy paper and sweet scent, was much superior to the books from Indian publishers found in the Indian bookstores. Chetan collected the Russian books and showcased all of them proudly on the shelf in his room.

The two world leaders were busy in tit-for-tat politics. And, March 1984 began with a bang. TV news covered reciprocating nuclear tests, first in Semipalatinsk and later in Nevada. The United States attacked Nicaragua. To raise the tensions, a Soviet submarine and USS aircraft carrier *Kitty Hawk* rammed into each other during a US exercise with South Korea. The whole incident was blamed on the incompetence of the Soviet sub-commander.

Sports conflicts followed. On the heels of the US boycott of the Moscow Summer Olympics in 1980, the USSR announced the boycott of the Los Angeles Summer Olympics of 1984. More than sixty countries had not participated in the Moscow Olympics. Reciprocating, fifteen or so nations from the communist bloc decided not to join the 1984 Summer Olympics in LA. Reasons for nonparticipation ranged from political differences to questioning players' security. The rumors were that there would be stricter doping tests in the States, so Russia wanted an excuse not to join the games rather than face the embarrassment of getting its athletes disqualified. India was never a strong contender in any particular event, except for some hope in field hockey, but Doordarshan telecasted the daily coverage of the games, and Chetan and family watched diligently. The year 1980 Olympics had given India some

54

reason to celebrate, as they won the field hockey gold medal. But, with so many nations abstaining, the win was not as sweet. The hopes were high on the 1984 team to repeat the performance and remove that asterisk next to the 1980 win.

Among these ongoing tensions between the United States and the USSR, rumors swirled that the CIA, ISI, and KGB had gotten involved in the Punjab conflict. Was it too good an opportunity for these organizations to pass up? Things got murkier as the indoctrination machine started churning out views, opinions, and rumors from all sides. A slew of misinformation, distrust, and propaganda shrouded any semblance of truth. There were whispers that the Indian government was planning to attack the Golden Temple to drive insurgents out and people talked about Pakistan getting involved in the conflict. The thought of another war was unthinkable, but could one be avoided?

Young Chetan and his classmates assessed the situation, frequently debating who was more powerful, the USA or the Soviet Union. Who had more military, more nuclear weapons, and more aircraft carriers? It often came down to a single question: Where would you want to live if you had the chance?

Any place was better than home at that point, Chetan thought. He had already decided that he would move abroad, get his higher education there, and make a ton of money. So much money that he would never have to suppress his desire to own things such as a remote-controlled car. He'd always wanted a remote-controlled car, but it was too expensive. He had seen one at his friend's place but never dared to ask his parents for one. He never wanted them to feel horrible for saying no.

"I would rather go and study in the US," Chetan would say.

"But Russia has a better engineering and science program," someone in the class would opine.

"But all their studies are in Russian. You'll spend the first two years just learning the language."

"So, what? They give scholarships for you to learn Russian. In Delhi, the Russian embassy offers lessons for free."

These conversations were a happy intermission for Chetan, transporting him out of scary Punjab and into the land of wonder and excitement. He dreamed of a day when he could leave the anguish and fear of living in Punjab and live in a rich, powerful, and strong country. A place where you could freely travel, stay out at night, and ride the buses and trains without the fear of getting killed. The USA was the first choice, and the second was West Germany. For Chetan, West Germany was the best country to study engineering. Among his prized possessions was the Staedtler geometry set.

"Well, you'll have to learn German."

"Yes, but that is not very hard. I heard it is very similar to Sanskrit, and Indians pick it up quickly," Chetan responded. "I can go to Max Muller Bhawan in Delhi and learn it in a few months."

Chetan's dad had been to West Germany. He told him fascinating stories: how clean the country was and how disciplined the Germans were. Vijay used to tell Chetan about the pride Germans had in their tools and machines and how much fun they had. The evening parties, beer gardens, touring the city on the weekends, dining out in the restaurants— Germans could do all the things that Chetan wished he could, but in 1980's Punjab, that kind of life was just a dream. Danger lurked everywhere. Nothing, and no one, was safe.

Chetan would get a much-needed escape when a friend

would invite him to watch a movie. Very few people had access to VCRs—video cassette recorders. Families with VCRs got those from their foreign trips to either Singapore, Abu Dhabi, or Hong Kong. The National VCR was the top-selling model and the pride of a family. It had so many buttons and options that you could never master that beast. The earlier model had a remote control that had a six-foot wire attached to it. The wireless VCR remote was not yet available. Chetan's father did not get one from his trip to Germany. German stores did not carry National VCRs, which they considered to be of poor quality, and the Grundig VCR cost too much.

Even though the school's final exams were right around the corner, one of Chetan's friends, Sanjay, got the newly released *Police Academy* film and called him.

"Hey, want to come over for a movie?"

"Can we meet on Sunday morning? Can we watch it then?" Chetan asked. Going out in the evening was not a great idea.

"No, we must return the cassette in a couple of hours."

"Okay, let me ask my mother."

Chetan told his parents he needed to complete some notes for school and rode his Hero bicycle to Sanjay's place to watch the movie. They watched forty minutes of it—the movie print was terrible, and it was the kind of English Chetan found hard to comprehend. Moreover, his mind was preoccupied by the anxiety of the ride back home. It was not recommended to be alone outside late in the evenings.

"I must leave now," he said. "I need to finish the homework, as well."

Chetan left Sanjay's and pedaled fast to reach home—the sun was setting. Chetan had to hurry to get home before dark. He did not want his Mom to worry.

Renu would get concerned if the boys were outside the house for more than an hour, especially late in the evenings. Riding his bicycle in the dark and then getting home late and receiving a healthy dose of beating from his mother was something that he wanted to avoid at any cost. His homework was not completed either. He cursed himself for leaving home for the stupid movie.

What was I thinking?

What am I going to say to Mom?

I think I can finish the homework in thirty minutes. I have enough time. It's just a few pages of writing.

I should not have gone out today.

Chetan reached home close to six thirty. Dad had still not returned, and Mom paced. Realizing she was distracted, Chetan quickly snuck into his room and started with his homework. She did not ask him about his visit to his friend. She had just finished preparing dinner and had hot water ready for Vijay's tea. Today was his turn to drive. Dad used to go to the office in a carpool with three colleagues. They switched every two days. It was not unusual for Vijay to arrive late, but seldom more than a half hour—otherwise, he'd call. The office was just seven miles from home.

Chetan continued finishing his homework and watched his mother pacing from room to room.

"Did Papa call?" she asked.

"No," he responded, sitting in his room. He wanted to stay far from her and tried to look busy with his studies. It was best to avoid her when she was stressed out.

"I do not know why he did not bother calling if he was getting late. He better not be stopping for challi!" Renu grumbled loudly to herself.

Dad and his colleagues once a while stopped on the way to pick up some challi–roasted corn–on the roadside. Chetan hoped that it would be something as simple as that. Shootings and attacks were escalating.

"Do you want me to call Ghosh Uncle's home?" Chetan offered. He was getting worried as well. Mr. Ghosh, Dad's carpool partner, was dropped first. "Maybe Aunty knows if they are running late."

"No, no need."

The curt response was driven by her ego. Renu would feel worse if Mrs. Ghosh knew about the delay, and she did not. Renu returned to the kitchen to start making the tea—something to keep her mind away from all the negative thoughts.

Soon enough, Chetan heard the car horn. It came from their '72 Fiat. Vijay pressed the horn every time he was at the street corner, just about to enter the street. That was a signal for Chetan to run and open the gates for the car to enter the premises. If he got to the gate in time, his Dad would not have to wait and would seamlessly roll the car into the driveway and park it in the garage.

Relief cut through the tension in the house. Chetan had a smile on his face, but Renu still looked grim, searching for answers. As soon as Vijay entered the home, the tea was served, and Chetan delivered the newspaper to Vijay.

"So, what happened?" Renu asked.

"Nothing, the tire got punctured," Vijay responded.

"Maybe you should think about getting a new car."

"Maybe. Maybe after the next promotion. There will be an extra car allowance."

One more day was in the books. It seemed a small victory

that all were back safe inside the home. Chetan returned to his room, picked up a paper and pencil, and started drawing some sketches. Vijay settled in his bedroom chair, reading the newspaper, feet up on the stool, with the TV running in the background.

6

Vijay Malhotra

Vijay Malhotra was born in 1944 in British India, a few years before India gained its independence, and before British India was divided into India and Pakistan. After the partition, the city where he was born became a part of Pakistan. Fortunately for them, they did not have to go through the bloodbath endured by refugees who were moving from one side to the other during the India-Pakistan partition. Vijay's father had a job transfer, and the family moved in 1946 to Ferozepur, which was on the Indian side. The family escaped the carnage of the 1947 migration and carried on with their lives.

Vijay's father was a government employee with humble means, earning barely enough to raise a large family of seven children. Five sons and two daughters. The second to last of all children, Vijay was pampered by everyone in the family. He was brilliant, excelled in his studies, and consistently ranked at the top of his class. The family was cruising along with their lives when destiny suddenly threw a curveball at them. Vijay's father was traveling on an official trip and would be gone for a few days. A few days after he had left, a knock sounded on the door one late evening. Vijay's mother opened the door and was face-to-face with a uniformed police official.

"I am sorry to inform you that Mr. Malhotra died from sudden cardiac arrest."

Vijay's mother collapsed on the ground. His elder brothers pulled her in, and the calm evening turned into a storm of cries and wailing. The noise reached the neighbors, and people started to gather at Vijay's home. The body was on its way to Ferozepur via the next train. A few men from the neighborhood took the two eldest sons and left for the railway station to receive the body.

Vijay was ten; he stayed at home with his devastated mother and inconsolable sisters.

The responsibility to bring up Vijay's family and keep everyone together landed on his mother's shoulders; she was supported by her eldest son, who had just turned twenty-one. Vijay's mother ruled the family with an iron fist. She made sure that all kids were appropriately educated, and when the time came, her two daughters had a proper wedding. She made sure that she kept the family's dignity and name intact. The pension was just 150 rupees a month.

To their credit, each child carried his or her weight, got scholarships, did reasonably well at school, and became a successful professional. Expectations of Vijay were high, though. He was considered the most intelligent of them all. Vijay was a math wizard and took immense pride in his schoolwork. Every homework assignment he submitted was done in immaculate handwriting. There were never any ink smudges on his notebooks. He kept his notebooks clean, covered in brown paper dust jackets. The eldest brother took him under his wing, started supporting his education, and paved a path for Vijay that took him to the top of the corporate world.

After his father's death, Vijay continued his education in Ferozepur and showed extraordinary potential to excel. His eldest brother challenged him and encouraged him to be the best in his studies. Vijay had decided that he would become an engineer, just like his eldest brother. He took every test and every school exam as a step toward his ultimate goal and focused on excellence, completing one class after another with top honors. He knew that education was the only salvation, and there was no one but him who could do it for him. He was now obsessed with it. Nothing else mattered other than being better than the others. Vijay was not going to let his brother or his mother down.

The first big test of Vijay's life came when he was in the tenth grade. It was the first time students took the state board exams. Vijay prepared hard for those exams. Success in that exam was supposed to determine his destiny, an indication that he was good enough to continue studying science for the next two years to get into an engineering college. The eldest brother was more anxious than everyone to know the results. He got the news that the results had been computed and would be released in a week. He could not wait and took the bus to the state school board's office to get his hands on the results early. Holding Vijay's roll number on a paper slip in his hand, he went straight to the registrar's office and asked the clerks to check Vijay's result.

"Please let me know the position of this roll number," the brother said.

"We cannot do that. Wait another four days, and results will be in the newspaper," the clerk pushed back.

"Just check the top ten and tell me if he is there."

"No, we cannot check anything for you."

"How about just the top five? Let me know if this number is in the top five."

The clerk insisted that he could not give the result to him before it went public, but after long cajoling, he did a check, more out of curiosity. He walked to a dusty cabinet, pulled a large, thick, leather-bound register, and opened it away from everyone's eyes. He was moving his finger up and down the page and then just stopped. When he turned around, his eyes were bigger, and his face had a mischievous smile. He still did not give him the result, but he did give him what he wanted.

"Yes, I have checked. *Mubarak ho*, he is in the top five. Congratulations!"

Vijay's brother was ecstatic. He immediately turned back, took the next bus home, and shared the news with everyone. Now, it was the waiting game to see the actual rank.

It was Monday morning, at six o'clock, and the kids were still asleep. Vijay's mother had just started her morning routine and preparations for breakfast. There was a sudden knock on the door. They never had any visitors. Not this early, anyway.

"Who is it?" Vijay's mother asked from behind the door.

"This is Vijay's principal from the school."

"Is everything okay? Is he in trouble?" she inquired, still behind the door, taking a second look at her clothes before opening the door.

"Yes, he is in big trouble," the principal replied. There were a few seconds of silence, and then he belted out a loud laugh.

Vijay's mother opened the door and saw the principal with a big smile on his face and a plate in his hand filled with some gurh, kishmish, and badam. His big belly moved as he continued to laugh.

"*Mubarak ho!* Vijay has gotten the first position!" he said. "No sweet shop was open this early, so I just got this gurh-kishmish."

"First in the school?" she asked.

"I would not come and wake you up so early if he was first in just the school. That we all knew already!" the principal joked. "He is first in the whole state board!" The principal handed the plate full of jaggery, resins, and almonds to Vijay's mother.

By this time, the others were up. One kicked Vijay, who was still asleep.

"Wake up! You have topped the board!"

Vijay leaped out of his bed, and the whole family jumped and ran around the house.

The principal continued his belly laugh and told the mother they were planning a procession the next day to celebrate the big achievement. It was a big deal for the school and the city. No one from the city had ever topped the state board exam.

After a quick breakfast, Vijay ran to his elder brother, who was beyond thrilled. His younger brother was his pride. Taking a little advantage of the situation, Vijay asked, "Phapa Ji, can I take your cycle out today?" Vijay looked at him, asking for the one and only cycle in the house. The eldest brother had the rights over it.

"Yes, go out and play with your friends," the brother said, beaming with pride.

The next day, the school principal picked Vijay up from home, situated him on a tractor-trolley, and stood right next to him. Vijay was proudly wearing his white shirt and khaki shorts. Dozens of visitors came and placed marigold garlands around Vijay's neck, and the procession started. The school and a couple hundred students, parents, teachers, and neighbors joined the parade for the Ferozepur kid who stood first in the state board exam.

Vijay continued on his path to success, got selected into an engineering college, and completed his degree. He never wanted to join a government job like his father or his elder brother. He wanted his efforts to be well recognized and rewarded. He wanted to join a private enterprise where he could rise on merit and not merely based on tenure.

He moved around the country for jobs, first in Jaipur, then Mumbai, and after a few rough starts, he finally found an opportunity in Patiala, Punjab. He began working for one of India's leading manufacturing powerhouses. For the first time, he started enjoying this work, and that showed in the results. He became the golden boy of the company. Vijay specialized in machine design. Designing and developing new machines and tools for factories was his passion. No matter how intricate the product was, Vijay would find a way to design a machine to produce it. Along the way, he was also learning the ways of the corporate world, winning hearts with his hard work, and always accepting every new challenge. He was a young lad whose mind was so sharp that no technical or administrative issue was too complex for him. He was a problem solver in every work situation.

His rise continued.

One of Vijay's managers saw an eligible bachelor in him and introduced him as the prospective groom to one of his family friends. One thing led to another, and the match was fixed. Renu and Vijay got married and settled down in Patiala.

However, marriage was nothing like either of them had

expected. Vijay was not ready for the commitment that marriage demanded and found it difficult to find time for Renu in his workaholic way of life. Anything that took his attention away from his work was a distraction. Their marriage had a rocky start. He did not understand why Renu was always irritated and why she kept pulling him away from his work to help with household tasks. He gave her the freedom to do as she desired, and he wanted to be left alone to focus on his work.

Vijay did not enjoy any romantic conversations, especially when his mother was around him. Renu's insistence on going out or making attempts at seeking affection from him grated him. He did not understand that the marriage between them was a shock for Renu as well, who hailed from a much more affluent family. Any instance where Renu talked about her parents' home and her life before marriage would hurt Vijay's ego. He grew tired of the constant fights between Renu and his mother. It took Renu almost four years to get to a state where she started to accept her fate, reconcile with the situation, and build a home they all wanted to live in. It was the time after Chetan's younger brother Vikki was born.

Vikki's birth brought some stability to the family. Vijay's mother had moved out to live with Vijay's elder brother, a win for Renu. A short while after, Vijay bought his first car. Even though it was a used black Fiat, Renu did not feel as embarrassed as when she sat pillion on a scooter. The car brought some redemption. They traveled to all their relatives in Ludhiana and then to Ferozeupr, Renu's maternal home, to show them their Fiat. The car brought the family together.

In addition to his reputation of being extremely intelligent, Vijay was known for his humility. In the office, his colleagues would sing praises about his down-to-earth nature.

"We have never seen such a gentle person. A humble soul."

"He is so dedicated at work. Look at the sacrifices he has made for the company."

"Look, he has not taken a day off in three years."

The more people praised him for his humility and sacrifice, the more obliged he felt to do more. It was a vicious cycle that weighed heavily on their marriage. His success came at a cost his family had to pay.

"If you are so obsessed about your work, you shouldn't have married," Renu used to complain.

"If you want to be like your father, make sure you do not marry. You have no right to ruin someone else's life," Renu often said to Chetan after her fights with Vijay.

Vijay was not a person who was particularly good at handling confrontations. He had extreme pride in his work and his convictions. He never took criticism well and never bothered to confront it, either. On occasions when he was reprimanded in the office, he would take all his frustration out at home. He never had the courage or even the skills to pick a fight, so all he could manage was his passive-aggressive behavior toward Renu and the kids.

"Let's have dinner," Renu said.

"No, I do not want to eat," replied Vijay, avoiding the conversation.

"Why? What happened?"

"Nothing. I have a migraine."

"You were okay this morning."

"Yes, it started just now. Let me sleep."

Renu and the kids were used to the sudden onset of Vijay's migraines. If Renu ever suggested that he speak up at his office or stand up for what he believed was right, his ego would take a big blow. No one could tell him what to do, especially how to be a man. Chetan's foundation was built by looking at Vijay.

Vijay's office was his place of worship, everything to him. Everyone there appreciated his work, and he gained the reputation of being the best machine designer in the firm. He got fast-tracked into a series of promotions. He was now deputy manager, heading the design group of a large manufacturing unit of one of the leading corporations in India. Endless days and nights spent at the office and on the manufacturing floor did not go unnoticed. His name and reputation reached the headquarters, and he was often called to New Delhi for various new and expansion projects. He was on the move, taking on bigger projects and newer challenges and becoming increasingly disconnected from Renu, Chetan, and Vikki.

His company selected Vijay to travel to West Germany for training. It was a rare honor extended only to very talented employees. The day Vijay got the news, the whole family celebrated. It was one of the rare occasions they went out for dinner. That was in 1982. The first person he called was his elder brother, who was as proud as ever. Vijay was the first person in the family to visit a foreign country. Vijay was also the first one to travel by plane when he first visited Bangalore. With each accomplishment, he became more dear to his elder brother. Many of his colleagues visited his home to congratulate him. There was a party at home to celebrate the upcoming foreign trip. Renu was happy to see some festivities at home, and the kids were busy making a list of things they wanted Vijay to bring back from Germany.

With his rise, his responsibilities at the office grew as well.

So did politics. He was pulled into union meetings, collective bargaining, negotiations, and dealing with the local politicians. Considered to be humble and respected by many, he would be pushed to go and negotiate with many unscrupulous leaders. He detested that work. He wanted to be left alone to focus on designing new machines, but this was the price to pay for his position. He became increasingly involved with working with the politicians and "contributing to the party funds," a euphemism for bribery.

The influence of these politicians increased even more during the eighties. Vijay had to make sure that they were on his company's side if business was to be done. He had to deal with the local goons to keep them happy, so they did not destroy the factory premises or prohibit the workers from entering at the behest of some strike. Many payouts were made to several political outfits, local leaders, and union leaders, just to keep the business running during the unrest in Punjab.

Vijay was out of his element. The work that he once loved became a burden. Corruption defiled his place of worship. And soon, that place was going to be desecrated. There would be blood, and it had been a long time coming.

7

April 1984: And. . . the Blood Flows

April was a special month for Chetan. Final exams were done, and a well-deserved break occurred before the next school year started. And, it was Chetan's birth month.

However, Chetan was extra excited this year, and not just because his eleventh birthday was coming. India was sending its first man into space! Amid so much political unrest, fear, and carnage, this unprecedented event brought the nation together. The first man from India to go to space gave people something new to talk about and something to be proud of. Indian air force pilot Rakesh Sharma was selected to be the first Indian to be sent into space. He was a part of the Soviet Interkosmos program.

On April 3, Chetan and his family were glued to their TV set as Delhi Doordarshan telecast the liftoff. Rakesh Sharma, along with Soviet cosmonauts, flew into space on *Soyuz T-11*, and the country erupted in celebration. This was a big event for the whole nation. Everyone watched the moment when Rakesh Sharma made a phone call from space to the prime minister, broadcasted repeatedly on the television.

Prime Minister Indira Gandhi asked him, *"Upar se Bharat kaisa dikhta hai aapko—How does India look from above?"*

Rakesh Sharma quoted poet Iqbal's line, *"Saare jahaan se achcha—Best in the whole world."*

And tears of pride flowed across the nation. No one knows whether the conversation was spontaneous or rehearsed, but it was appropriate. It was a momentous time that made the whole country proud. Chetan, Vikki, and Vijay clapped, overwhelmed by the event. The room was charged with emotion. Chetan could not have asked for a better birthday present.

As the school break came to an end, Vijay and Chetan got their "desert coolers" ready for the summer. Servicing the cooler was an exciting ritual every summer. Over the weekend, Chetan helped Vijay to replace the evaporative dried grass-wood-wool pads in the cooler. This time, they paid a little extra to get superior *khus*, poppy husk pads that emitted a sweet smell when water dripped through them. Chetan first experienced the *khus* smell during his last visit to his grandparents' house. He insisted Vijay buy the same pads this year. Chetan was surprised that Vijay easily agreed. Chetan felt rich. The very first run of the cooler was so thrilling. The smell of the water dripping on the fresh *khus* husk pads for the first time can only be beaten by the *sondhi* smell, the petrichor of the first monsoon raindrops falling on the dry land. Chetan would have to wait a few more days for his first night's sleep with the cooler.

It was a day like any other. Vijay got ready for the office. He ate breakfast a bit early, as it was his turn to drive. Vijay liked to drive in a carpool, as it took the monotony away from the drive and also saved petrol. He finished his usual breakfast of a plain paratha and a steel glass full to the brim with doodh-chai, a sweet black tea made only with milk. The kids were getting ready for school as well. Renu was busy giving them breakfast and packing their lunch.

Now a senior manager, Vijay pulled out his newer car, another Fiat. Though secondhand, this one was in a much better condition than his first. The previous owner had hardly driven the car. He was an old gentleman who did not drive the car at all and ultimately decided to part ways with it. Vijay got a good deal and was really happy with his purchase. It was of a strange green color, somewhere between lime and fern. No one liked the color initially, but they all eventually got used to it.

It was a bright April morning, but the air was still cool. Vijay started on his route and picked up Sardar Amrik Singh, Sardar Amrinder Singh, and a Bengali colleague, Mr. Tapan Ghosh, from their homes and was on the way to the office. He stopped at the Grewal Petrol Station to fill the car and continued on his route to pick up the three colleagues. Each one of them was standing outside their houses as Vijay picked them up. He enjoyed the lively discussions while driving to the office and did not mind some cross-banter during those conversations. Office politics and upcoming elections were routine topics. However, the topic of elections was always a tense one, not because of different political affiliations but because of the terror elections could bring, the strikes and violence they instigated, and the impact they had on their jobs. Before they knew it, they were at the doors of the big office campus. The whole journey took about twenty-five minutes.

The four of them were not ready for what awaited them;

things in Patiala were going to get ugly. The horror would come close to home, and Vijay would witness the carnage up close. He would have to see it with his eyes open. He would not have the option to run away or look away.

Vijay's office campus was a large twenty-acre compound with ten-foot boundary walls topped with razor wire. Security was on high alert. In addition to the private security guards who checked identity cards for all, a few police guards were stationed there as well. But all this was just a farce in the name of security. The security guards in front of the gates made minimum wage. They were not trained to manage any escalated law-and-order situation and could offer no deterrence in those situations.

As Vijay's car rolled in front of the main green gate, the security guard looked into the car and gave Vijay a cursory salute. Then, the guard pulled out a long pole with a mirror on the end that he slid under the vehicle to see if any explosives were hidden under the car. The security guard was quite casual about it, having done that to dozens of cars that morning. He waved to the guy inside, who opened the gate and let the car in. Vijay drove the car toward the building and dropped his passengers, Amrik, Amrinder, and Tapan. Vijay then continued to drive toward the parking lot, located his assigned spot, parked his car, and started walking to his office. The parking area was a five-minute walk from the main office building.

Suddenly, chaos ensued. Screaming. Yelling. Pushing. People running all over the place. Vijay could not make any sense of it. Right in front of the main building, something had just happened, exactly where he'd dropped his three carpool friends.

Vijay started running toward the crowd. As he was running, screams made it clear that someone was stabbing people.

"Malhotra Sahib, don't go to that side. Get inside your car!"

"Malhotra Sahib, two people are stabbed."

"Malhotra Sahib, come fast. Take a look."

More than three thousand people worked there. Vijay was moving fast toward the location of the incident. Upon arrival, his mouth hung open.

Two men were lying on the ground, in a pool of blood— Amrik and Amrinder. Amrik was not moving at all. His white striped shirt had turned red, soaked with blood. His hands and legs were spread apart, and one shoe was off his foot. His mouth was wide open, as if he was still trying to scream, but his voice was not coming out.

Amrinder was twitching, making some gurgling sounds. His turban was off his head and lying next to him. His hand would move up as if pointing to something, but no one could figure out what he was trying to say. Vijay dropped to his knees, right beside them. He shook Amrik. No response. Amrinder's breathing was getting weak as well.

"Get the ambulance from the dispensary and pull up the office car. Take them to the Rajendra Hospital!" Vijay screamed. He looked around frantically. "Where is Tapan?"

"He is around the side of the building. He was running toward that side." Someone pointed toward a corner.

And Vijay started running toward the side of the building. As he turned around the corner of the building, he saw another group of people surrounding Tapan. He was standing, holding his stomach tight.

"Oh my God! Are you okay, Mr. Ghosh?" Vijay tried talking to him.

Tapan was not speaking. Too shocked to talk. He was limping with his arms around the shoulders of two people. One person had taken his turban off and wrapped it around Tapan's stomach to stop blood flow. Someone had stabbed Tapan as well.

"Mr. Malhotra, please call home. He stabbed me. He stabbed me, Mr. Malhotra," Tapan said as he finally realized Vijay was there. "Please take me to the hospital."

"Yes, the ambulance is coming."

There was only one ambulance available on the campus. The office workers put Amrik and Amrinder in there and took them to the hospital. Waiting for another one to arrive would take too much time. The chaos continued, and police were running around, trying to apprehend the culprit. Security sirens were blowing in every building of the campus, indicating workers to stop the work. Everyone was rushing toward the main gate to get out of the campus. Fortunately, the company car with its driver was available; Vijay and another person jumped into the car with Tapan and rushed him to the hospital.

Vijay brought Tapan straight to the emergency room and then used the hospital pay phone to call Tapan's wife. The company car was already on its way to pick her up. Tapan was in the surgery room, and Vijay was pacing outside. After a couple of hours at the hospital, Vijay left for the office to pick up his car.

He drove back home. Alone. This morning, he had three people in the car with him, and now, a few hours later, he was returning home all alone. He tried to remember their conversations from the morning, the jokes, the banter, the laughter. He reached home but waited several minutes inside the car. Finally, he exited. It was about noon. He opened the gate and pulled the car inside.

"What happened? Why are you home so soon? Did you forget something?" Renu asked, clearly surprised by his arrival.

Vijay's face was pale, his eyes were red, and his hands shaking. He was crying on the way back home but tried to hold his tears back when he saw Renu.

"A worker stabbed Amrik, Amrinder, and Tapan. Tapan is in the hospital. His wife is there."

Renu's heart pounded in her chest as she absorbed the shocking news. Her eyes widened in disbelief as the words washed over her. The color drained from her face, leaving behind a pallor that mirrored the stark gravity of the news, and her hands trembled as they involuntarily reached for support.

"What? What about others?" She somehow collected herself and asked.

"They are dead. Amrik died instantly, and Amrinder died on his way to the hospital." Vijay's throat was dry.

Tears began to flow from Renu's eyes. She did not know Amrik or Amrinder well but had met Tapan and his wife at many company parties. She was terrified. The violence reached so close to home. Vijay was quiet and still. The only noise you could hear was Renu sobbing. It was almost time for the kids to return from school. She was trying her best to gather herself.

"Let me make some food for Mrs. Ghosh," Renu offered.

"Sure. We'll leave for the hospital once the kids come back." Vijay tried hard to keep his composure. He looked away, walked toward the phone in the bedroom, and started making calls.

Once Chetan and Vikki arrived from the school, Renu gave

them food. She ran upstairs to inform the landlady about the incident.

"We are going to the hospital and will return in a few hours. Please keep an eye on the kids."

They left for the hospital.

As Vijay entered the hospital from the emergency ward entrance, he saw hundreds of office workers still waiting outside, not because they cared about Tapan but because they were too shocked to go back to their homes. Many went straight to the hospital from the office. They were together so that they could share their fears, their feelings, and their anger. Police constables were situated around the hospital to make sure that the situation did not escalate and instigate any more violence.

Tapan was still in the operating room, but the doctors assured Vijay and Tapan's wife that he would survive. Apart from his wife, Tapan did not have any relatives in Patiala. His whole family resided in Calcutta. The doctors asked Vijay to arrange for more blood. Fortunately, there was no shortage of donors. Hundreds from the office lined up to donate their blood. Vijay was one of the donors. Surgeons had to remove Tapan's severely damaged kidney, but he survived.

Vijay was broken. He kept wondering if he were not the driver, he could have been the one stabbed to death. He was scared to go to the office but somehow pushed himself to be there for his work and for his people. There was no counseling available for the families and friends who had just gone through an unimaginable tragedy. No professional help was available to guide them on dealing with PTSD, not for the family of the deceased, not for Tapan, not for Vijay. The term PTSD was not commonly understood or accepted. So, everyone had to bear the cross and deal with the trauma in their own way.

A few days later, police apprehended the attacker. He was a factory worker who had gotten involved with some radical group a while back. No eyewitness came forward to testify against him. Vijay did not speak for days after the incident. Renu understood. The hospital was the last place anyone would see Tapan or his wife. Once Tapan was discharged from the hospital, he wrapped up his household in Patiala and returned to his native home in Calcutta, without saying any goodbyes.

Chetan knew what had happened, and the fear gnawed at him. Chetan prayed that his daily trips to school go without any incident. He prayed every day that his father would come back home safely. Chetan picked up new rituals of lining his shoes straight without touching each other. He walked in a way so that he did not step on the lines on the floor. He would pray every time there was a plane in the sky, to save it from crashing.

His obsessive behavior cemented into his core. He felt he could gain control of his world by maintaining this kind of order. In his mind, all these rituals would save him, his family, and the people around him. The violence that was close to home had seeped deep into his psyche. A peaceful world was a far-fetched dream when the blood flowed so close to home, and all he could do was pray to survive another day. He wished for a day when these senseless killings would stop, and he could roam around and play without any fear. However, those days were far away. Things were only going to get worse before they got better.

8

May 1984: Elections Are Coming

No matter how shaken by turmoil, humans somehow manage to pull themselves back up and carry on. Memories tend to be short-lived, and life gets busy.

Vijay and family returned to their daily routines of school, office, homework, meetings, and TV. Visits to friends continued for a few days to support each other, and then talks about the office killings became less frequent. Even in Vijay's office, after just a few weeks, work returned to normal. Targets need to be met, and Vijay had to make up for the lost days of production.

With Chetan and Vikki at school and Vijay at the office, Renu felt even more isolated inside the home after the killings at her husband's office. The rare occasions when they ventured out to the market or to a friend's house for a Saturday night dinner no longer existed. Renu wanted a break but had no idea how to have that conversation with Vijay.

One evening, after Vijay's return from the office, she hesitantly brought it up.

"It's been weeks sitting at home. Let's go see a movie," Renu proposed.

She had one in mind. *Sharaabi*, the big blockbuster starring megastar Amitabh Bachchan and Jaya Prada, was just released. The movie snobs rejected the film, saying it was a copy of an American movie, *Arthur*, but the general public still flocked to it. The movie was about the son of a rich father, Vicky Kapoor, who grew to be an alcoholic because of the lack of love from his father. The protagonist, played by Amitabh, was brought up by a caretaker and ultimately was brought back on track and saved by the love he got from a dancer, Meena. A lot of drama happens in between, before they come together for a happily-ever-after ending. It was a typical Hindi *masala* movie, but Amitabh Bachchan and Jaya Prada, with all the superhit songs, dances, and comedy, kept bringing people back for more. Radio incessantly played songs from the film and crowds all over India kept coming to watch the movie. The public was awed by the film and stormed theaters across the nation. The movie was almost unavoidable. Although, in Punjab the situation was different. The theaters were running almost empty.

"A movie?" Vijay asked as he lowered his newspaper, looking at Renu. His face was turning red, and his lips were pressing hard, as if working hard to stop the words from coming out. "Do you think this is a good time? It's not even been a month. What do you think people will say when they see you outside the theater?" With each sentence, his voice rose and became increasingly stern.

The murders in the office were still fresh in Vijay's mind. To be seen outside, enjoying a movie, seemed unthinkable for Vijay. Patiala was a small city, and if he went out for a movie,

81

people would certainly come to know. He had to maintain the image that he cared for his people and was with them in the time of their sorrows.

This was one of the few times Chetan heard Vijay raise his voice in front of Renu. Usually, he avoided confrontation.

"It was just a thought…." Renu trailed. "Never mind." She crossed into the kitchen.

Chetan stayed quiet in his room. Dad was easily irritated those days. Every time he found Chetan, he asked him about his studies and, no matter the response, Dad found a reason to be angry with him. And this would give Renu yet another excuse to lash out at Chetan.

The boy kept his head down in his room, pretending to read his school notes. But all the talk about the movies had him thinking about the new American movie that everyone in the class was talking about, the international blockbuster *Indiana Jones and the Temple of Doom*.

Chetan had heard a lot of talk in school about all the action in the Indiana Jones movie. Moreover, the big evil man in the movie, the villain, was an Indian, Amrish Puri, who played the role of Mola Ram. Most kids couldn't have cared less about the hero, Harrison Ford; all the talk centered on Amrish Puri acting in a Hollywood movie. However, many Indian newspapers publicly castigated the movie for stereotyping Indians in Hollywood. Some even criticized Amrish Puri for accepting a role that degraded Indians by showing them eating monkey brains, performing human sacrifice, and showing a white man yet again as the savior. The Indian government also filed a complaint to ban the movie. Nevertheless, the movie was a global box office hit.

Chetan was not concerned with the controversy and wondered if he could slide out one of these days to his friend Sanjay's place and see the movie. Getting out of the house and visiting friends outside the neighborhood was almost unthinkable. He did not ask.

The routine killings in Punjab continued. Often, the victims were Hindus, but Sikh casualties happened as well. Dinnertime with family became increasingly tense. Dinner was accompanied by TV news, which was filled with incidents about murders and curfews. The month of May saw an increase in violence across the state. The television ran news about a politician who was killed in Ferozepur, and that led to another wave of sectarian violence, resulting in several other deaths. The news of authorities enforcing curfew in various cities, police raiding multiple houses, and capturing men carrying assault weapons was becoming common.

The regular coverage of crossfire between police and insurgents and police claiming wins as they paraded surrendered men in front of the press became everyday news. Ferozepur, Renu's parent's house, had become a hotbed of activity. It was close to the Pakistan border, and frequent arms and personnel infiltration across the India-Pakistan border occurred near that area. Chetan wondered if it would even be possible to visit his grandparents during summer vacation.

Staying home was Chetan's only option. Watching TV did not provide any reprieve either. It was all about death and destruction. Except on May 23, when Bechandri Pal created history. She became the first Indian woman mountaineer to conquer Mount Everest—a feat she accomplished a day before her thirtieth birthday. It gave Chetan a reason to rejoice. Even with all the chaos, there were slight glimmers of hope, a few occasions for celebration, and he wanted to hold onto

83

those moments that brought him joy. As Chetan watched the news, he beamed, reflecting the enthusiastic smiles of the newscasters, who were also enjoying a break from their usual somber faces as they covered death and destruction.

The phone rang. Chetan answered it.

"Hello!"

"Namaste, Chacha Ji," Chetan greeted his uncle—Dad's younger brother, Ravi.

"Namaste, beta. God bless you," said Ravi. "Is Papa at home?"

"Yes, Papa is here. I'll call him." Chetan moved the receiver from his face and shouted, "Papa, it's Chacha Ji on the phone."

Vijay walked over to his room and took the phone. Chetan sat beside him, eagerly listening and hoping the call was about his uncle visiting them. Even better, he may be inviting them to come to Ludhiana. Ravi and his wife loved Chetan and Vikki as their children. They had a small house, and during their visits, Chetan, Vikki, and cousins would sleep on a couple of mattresses on the floor. Chetan cherished those moments.

"Hello! How are you? How is everyone at home?" Vijay asked with a smile.

"Oh. Oh no." The smile on Vijay's face quickly faded. He sat down on the chair next to the phone table.

"Yes. Do not worry. Yes. Give me the numbers." Vijay's hands trembled as he noted numbers on a piece of paper. His face was grim.

"Yes, I have noted the number of your insurance policies. Don't worry. Everything will be okay." And he set the phone down.

Mom had entered the room and stood next to Dad.

"What happened?"

"Nothing—yet. Ravi has been assigned to election duty."

84

Vijay's head was hanging low as he looked at his clasped hands.

Any local, village, or state election became a ticking time bomb. Conducting elections was not without peril. Even in the middle of tight police security and army presence, the polling booths were attacked. Booth captures, coercion, theft of poll boxes, inciting fear, and even bomb attacks were common occurrences.

The year 1984 was the year of the eighth Indian general election. The last election was in 1980, and the Indian National Congress took the majority of votes, bringing Indira Gandhi back to power. Indira's position and her hold on the masses were at stake during the upcoming election. The Congress Party was pulling all the levers to secure another win. The elections were in December, and the campaign activity was in full force.

Elections required a lot of manpower, and usually, government officials were assigned to election duties to manage the election booth and count votes. Vijay's brother Ravi, the youngest of the seven siblings, was employed by a government bank and was assigned to supervise a voting station in a nearby village. Assignment to election duty could be a death sentence. Anyone leaving for election duty was sent off by family as if going into a war. Election duty brought a somber mood, with prayers for the safe return of the family member. Vijay's brother had begun making his contingency plans, which included calling Vijay to let him know where his life insurance policies were, what bank accounts he had, and the location of his bank lockers. It was common for husbands leaving for election duty to make such preparations, providing wives with a list of people to contact if something happened. Even young kids were apprised of their parents' pensions and provident funds and who they should live with in case something happened to their caretakers.

Vijay kept his brother's insurance policy numbers in his closet. Vijay did not work for the government and was not required to go for any election duty. However, he also had to make preparations at the office and at home. He had regular meetings in the office to plan work during the months of elections and their readiness in case of any violence. Vijay routinely met with various political leaders, trying to gauge who could win the elections. His company wanted to ensure the favor of the new government. With the recent murders at the office, everyone was on the edge about the elections.

Vijay, too, followed the drill of preparing the family. He sat down with Renu and Chetan, and they went through the financials, bank accounts, insurance policies, provident funds, and pension papers. Then, Vijay organized everything, put it in a file, and stored it in their steel almirah.

"How about you take the kids to Delhi for a few days during the elections?" Vijay asked Renu. Sending them to Ferozepur or even Ludhinana was equally dangerous. Delhi seemed to be a safer choice.

"You could stay with your sister or mine."

"Can you take some time off? So we all can go together. You have not taken a day off since last year," Renu replied. "I am not going alone," she insisted.

She was never one to run away in fear, and the thought of her leaving her husband to save her life was almost an insult.

"Taking time off doesn't seem possible. Too much going on at the office," Vijay replied. "Let's talk when the elections are near, and maybe I can figure something out then."

They went over the emergency plan again, covering scenarios, whom to call, where to go, and which paper to take to whom. Vijay trained and tested Chetan and Vikki constantly.

"What is the phone number for my office? What is Mama Ji's phone number?" Renu's brother was the first one they should call, and he would arrange whatever was needed.

"What is Chacha Ji's address?" Vijay's younger brother was the most reliable and loving of them all. For Chetan and Vikki, Chacha Ji's place was their second home. He and his wife would take good care of the boys if anything happened.

Strangely, these morbid rehearsals brought some relief to both Renu and Vijay. Every time they had this drill with the kids, they could sleep peacefully that night.

For Chetan, however, these tests and the constant fear of losing his parents proved agonizing. Whenever they discussed the phone numbers or where the files were, Vikki answered enthusiastically. He enjoyed getting all the numbers correct and getting kudos from his father for memorizing everything. Chetan, on the other hand, was older and understood the implications better than Vikki; so for Chetan, these drills were scary and painful and served only to push him further into anxiety, with a fear of the unknown gnawing at his heart.

Chetan was constantly vigilant, looking back while walking, avoiding eye contact with strangers, not leaving the house after dark, and chanting "Ram Ram" one hundred and eight times before sleeping. Anxiety and fear were becoming a part of his being, and his rituals to keep him away from the dread were becoming obsessive-compulsive.

Growing up in those times was like walking on eggshells all day, every day. Thoughts about losing his parents, being orphaned, or getting shot at on his way to school were sucking away his life and soul.

Sometimes, he wished to be hit by a bullet just to get it over with.

9

June 1984: Fire Ignites

How anyone could have survived Punjab in June 1984 is unfathomable. The epoch of fear, insecurity, and uncertainty engulfed every Punjab resident.

While the film *Ghostbusters* mesmerized the Western world, people in Punjab had their own demons to fight. And their fight was not make-believe. The fight, the guns, the blood that flowed in the streets, the thousands of deaths—they were all too real.

The situation in Punjab had been simmering for a while now. The apprehensions about the upcoming elections and anticipation of accompanying violence had made everyone nervous. The anxiety among people across the cities in Punjab was palpable. The undercurrents in political circles indicated that something ominous was about to happen. The onslaught of rumors was at an all-time high, and people were preoccupied with hypothetical arguments. Many expected that the ongoing government negotiations would bring some peace. But no one ever thought that they were about to witness one of the most shocking incidents of their lives.

On Friday, June 1, 1984, something unthinkable happened. Early sunrise ushered in a sweltering day. Vijay was going through his usual morning routine of finishing his morning tea, followed by a bath, and doing his puja in front of a mandir he created on a wall shelf in his room, where some photos and small idols of gods and goddesses were placed. However, an ominous feeling came over Vijay. The daily TV news and rumors about the government tightening its stronghold and going after insurgents before the elections made Vijay uneasy. He lit the incense stick with the smell of roses, pushed it into a silver lotus stand on the shelf, and completed his daily recital of "Hanuman Chalisa," an ode to Lord Hanuman. The sweet smell of rose perfume spread across the whole house, but it was not enough to ease Vijay.

After finishing his puja, he came out of his room and saw some commotion in the drawing room. Renu was sitting next to the radio that was now playing a washing powder jingle. Chetan and Vikki, still in their pajamas, stood at her side.

"What's happening? Why are you not ready for school?"

"Papa, put the TV on," Chetan said.

"TV? No TV so early in the morning. That is the only thing you ever want."

"No. See the news! The army has attacked the gurdwara!"

"What? Where did that happen?" Vijay asked.

"In Amritsar. The Golden Temple," Renu said, as though her fog had cleared.

Vijay steadied himself. "What? How is that possible?"

He had heard rumors that the government might send an army to Punjab to extract insurgents who had been living inside the gurdwara, but no one expected anything like this actually to happen. Sending the army into any gurdwara was not even considered a possibility, let alone into the most sacred of them all. Vijay turned the TV on, and the morning news was still talking about the Indian government dispatching the army to Sri Harminder Sahib Gurdwara, the Golden Temple, in Amritsar, Punjab, to capture the insurgents living inside the complex. The incident shook the entire state of Punjab.

The Indian army had launched Operation Blue Star, the code name of the military action on the Golden Temple, the holiest of Sikh temples, located in Amritsar, Punjab.

The government had implemented a total media and press blackout in Amritsar, and the rumor mill churned. People were hungry for more information, but no verifiable facts were available. The government suspended all city transportation services and enforced a curfew. It was a full-blown war situation in the city that military forces had taken over.

"The neighbor aunty says we should not go to school today," Chetan said, trying to convince Dad to let them stay home.

Chetan was not the one to make excuses to skip school, but today, he was scared. Renu picked up the phone and called the school, and yes, they had already decided to close till the situation got settled.

"So, it has started," Vijay mumbled.

He dreaded such a day would come. He started calling his colleagues who were wrapping up the night shift to understand the situation. And then, he got busy calling his office headquarters in Delhi. The unrest and violence were detrimental to the business. The business was already down for the last couple of years, and now this. He did not want to deal with the repercussions of the army attacks and the pressure of the upcoming elections. The situation for him

91

was going from bad to worse. Vijay was afraid of even more protests at the office and retaliation toward Hindu families across the city.

The first day of the attack started with military firing toward the Golden Temple complex to assess the powers they were against, and then slowly, by June 3, they surrounded the whole complex. The forces kept moving in, and a full-force attack started on June 5. Conflicting news emerged about whether the troops gave pilgrims enough time to vacate the temple premises or if they indiscriminately fired and killed anyone who stood in their way.

Chetan's school declared closure for the next seven days. He, Vikki, and Renu spent their time glued to the radio or television, hoping for new information about the situation in Amritsar. The national radio and TV channels were the only ways to get any news. The government had imposed a complete media blackout, and the journalists were not allowed to enter the city of Amritsar. The military had cut off all communication channels, including telephone lines and telegraph services, which meant it was nearly impossible to get any information about what was happening inside the temple complex. In addition, the government imposed a curfew in the city. The residents were confined to their homes and could not communicate with the outside world.

The situation in Amritsar remained shrouded in secrecy and speculation. Meanwhile, fear spread like wildfire across all other cities in Punjab as well. There were rumors of heavy fighting, with the military using tanks and artillery to flush out everyone inside the temple complex. There were reports of severe civilian casualties. The army operation was not limited to Amritsar. The army executed simultaneous attacks on many gurdwaras across the state.

The Golden Temple, a symbol of Sikhism and a revered pilgrimage site, had been desecrated, and there was a sense of deep sadness and anger among the Sikh community. People were outraged at the government's decision to use military force to resolve a political issue, and various political parties called for justice and accountability. The Hindu community living in Sikh-majority Punjab feared retaliation, and they were on high vigil.

Ferozepur, Renu's parents' home, was already a volatile city and was a target of military action as well. Attacks on gurdwaras in Ferozepur had put Renu's family in quite a precarious situation. Renu was extremely nervous. She frantically tried to call her parents, but the phone never connected. She was running down the list of all relatives and acquaintances in Ferozepur, but it was futile. Ferozepur was under a total press and communication blackout as well. The only piece of news you could get was from the government-run TV and radio stations. And soon, the military action reached close to home.

On the night of June 6, somber Patiala shook under the thunder of automatic assault rifles. Sudden popping, exploding sounds rattled the neighborhood. Vijay and Renu stopped what they were doing and tried to listen to what was happening outside. The commotion outside got louder. One by one, each neighbor came out of their homes. The gunfire was continuous but seemed to be coming from far away.

Realizing people were gathering on the streets, Vijay and Renu also cautiously stepped out to see what was happening. Chetan also sneaked out behind them. The noise came from the direction of the most prominent Sikh temple of Patiala,

Gurdwara Dukhniwaran Sahib (the Place that Removes all Sorrows).

Vijay, Renu, Vikki, and Chetan looked at the sky toward the gurdwara. Vijay's head was tilted backward, and his mouth wide open. Renu had her hands covering her mouth and her eyes glued to the horizon. Bright blue flares were lighting up the skies. On its own, it could have been a beautiful sight. Chetan had never seen such a thing in his life. Even the Dussehra fireworks in the Modi Mandir never went that high and never were that bright. Those Dussehra fireworks were a memory of the past. There hadn't been any Dussehra, Diwali, or Guru Purab fireworks in years. The blue flares were followed by many rounds of explosives and roaring guns. By this time, everyone from the neighborhood was out on the streets. Patiala, like other cities, was also under curfew orders, but standing in the streets within your neighborhood was usually not a problem—until you saw a military vehicle approaching, as that was a signal to rush back inside. There were frequent patrols by military vehicles across the city. The Army had complete powers to apprehend citizens and hand them to the police.

Everyone was looking at the sky in an eerie silence. The sky was changing colors with hues of blues and reds, something no one had ever seen. The only sounds were the popping of flare guns followed by the thunder of automatic weapons. The whole episode lasted for thirty-five minutes.

Finally, breaking the spell, Vijay pulled Chetan and Vikki back and asked Renu to get inside the house and lock the doors. Chetan's heart was beating unusually fast. He held onto his brother tight as they ran inside the house. This was the second time he had heard the sound of guns firing after New

Year's Eve. And this time, it was much scarier. Everything was so surreal. As if he were in the battle zone. His legs were trembling, and his back was sweaty, as if death brushed by him, and his fear reached new heights.

Chetan was back in his room but still tormented. Whispers from his parents' bedroom came to him, but he shut them out. He stared at the walls, hands clasped, as he tried to remember some prayer that could protect him and give him strength to cope with his fears. It took him hours before he could fall asleep.

Renu was still agitated the next day, augmented by the lack of news from her parents. She spent the day pacing around the house, restless, pretending to do some work. The kids were home, and so was Vijay. His office was shut down for a couple more days. The whole day was wrapped in strange silence across the house. Renu and Vijay were not talking much. Chetan and Vikki stayed in their rooms, pretending to study or to read their comic books. Once in a while, Renu visited her sons and reminded them to keep up with their studies, and they would nod. Her voice did not have the usual forceful authority.

The evening was spent inside the home as well. Renu feared running into their Sikh homeowners. She did not know how to face them. The kids were ordered to remain inside as well. Renu did not want neighbors to mistake the loud noise of kids playing outside as a disrespect to the grim situation at hand. It was getting dark, and dinner was ready, but no one wanted to eat. It was a day of mourning for most of the community. The desecration of the gurdwara and news of killings across the state weighed heavily on everyone's mind.

Renu went to Vijay. "Should I lay down the dinner for you?"

"No, I'll eat later. Get the kids to eat."

"Have a little," she said, making a half-hearted attempt.

Vijay ignored her. He was in no mood to eat. He was worrying about his office. The visions of the killings of his carpool friends were coming back to him and haunting him. He worried that the army attack on the gurdwaras would lead to more such incidents. He worried about going to the office in such a dangerous situation, but he had no choice. He had to work, and staying back home was not an option for him.

The lack of communication was building up frustration and anxiety for Renu. She had been trying to contact her parents for a few days now. Many neighbors were visiting them to use their phones to contact their relatives in Amritsar and other cities. Most were unsuccessful. People were desperate for information, but with no reliable sources available, they were forced to rely on rumors and gossip.

Then, suddenly, the phone bell rang. Vijay picked it up.

"Hello, who is this?" Vijay asked anxiously.

"Are you Vijay Malhotra?" the voice on the other side inquired.

"Yes."

"I am calling to tell you that your family is well in Ferozepur."

"But who are you, please?" Vijay asked while taking a deep sigh of relief.

"Renu's brother sent a message through one of his friends and asked us to call you. I am Hari Singh."

"Do you know Renu's family?"

"No, not personally. I just got a message to call you. Do not worry. They all are fine."

Some news is better than no news, Vijay thought.

"Many thanks for calling. I am highly obliged," he said and

put the phone down.

Renu sidled up next to him.

"All is well at home in Ferozepur," he said softly.

Renu's dam of tears broke. She sobbed uncontrollably, face buried in her hands.

"Have faith. God will make things right." Vijay looked away and tried to hold his tears back.

Everyone's life was turning upside down. The friends started to look at each other with suspicion. The community living together for decades was confronted with us versus them choices. Suddenly, religion determined allegiance and not decades-old friendships. What was Vijay supposed to do? Run from here? And where? This was where he belonged. His family was a mix of Hindus and Sikhs. Did he need to choose between relatives, his brothers? Everything was jumbled up for him. The pieces did not fit together, no matter how hard he tried. Real life was much more complex and brutal than the game of Tetris, released to the world this month. Only if the pieces of relationships, friendships, religion, work, and family could be rotated, twisted, and arranged as easily for everything to stack nicely.

The curfew continued. Food became more and more scarce. During the few hours of curfew suspension, people stormed ration shops, only to find them empty. Many neighborhoods were out of electricity for many days. Getting very basic supplies such as wheat flour, oil, and lentils required knowing someone who could help you locate the sellers stockpiling and selling the goods at a premium.

Having a familial connection in the army was an asset. An army officer could help to get some food, rice, eggs, onions, or tomatoes. Renu's cousin was a colonel in the army. He was not officially posted in Patiala, but his parents, Renu's aunt and uncle, lived in the city. One day, in the midst of curfew, he showed up at the door, fully uniformed and in his military Jonga. During the curfew, he decided to check on Renu. She was so relieved to see him, and Chetan felt an instant sense of security and peace. Seeing Renu relax made him happy—anything that could bring some serenity was indeed welcome. Renu's cousin brought four dozen eggs, a sack of potatoes, flour, and some oil. He dropped off the rations and left. He had to help a few more families and then return to his post.

Renu took a dozen eggs and some potatoes upstairs to the landlady. She intended to help her out, but it was also an attempt to extend a truce. Two families of different religions living in the same building could lead to confrontations. Tolerance was at its lowest, and it did not take much for people to explode and break into verbal or physical fights. As Renu climbed the stairs, each step felt like an anchor dragging her deeper into the abyss of guilt, and each stair echoed the pounding of her anxious heart. She rang the doorbell.

"Here is some food," Renu said softly as soon as Mrs. Randhawa opened the door.

Mrs. Randhawa looked at her. Her face was stern. The usual smile was absent, but there was no anger or hate either.

"Do you have enough for your home?" she inquired.

Renu nodded and looked away. Mrs Randhawa extended her two arms, and Renu placed the two polythene bags in her hands.

"When Sardar Ji goes to the market, we'll get some rations for you as well. Let me know what you need." She accepted the offering graciously. "Are you all doing okay?" she asked Renu.

"Yes."

"You and Malhotra Ji have nothing to worry about. Let me know if you need anything. You are safe here."

Renu came back trembling, drained of emotions; she wanted to cry but did not have enough energy.

The curfew was eventually relaxed and was limited to the nighttime. During the day, people could go out and continue their work. Offices opened, but there was nothing normal about it. Vijay's first day back to the office was declared a "Black Day" by the labor unions and local leaders. Attacks on holy places were condemned across the country.

The labor union at Vijay's office asked all employees to wear black turbans and black pants. It was the attire of mourning to demonstrate anger and resentment toward the government. People were expected to abide by the call and show their support for the protest. Vijay wore a white shirt with black pants that day. He wanted to join the show of solidarity within the community. He also wanted to avoid altercations with the union leaders who would confront him for not obeying the call. The memory of his friends' murders at the office had made him more cautious. In the office, Vijay avoided discussing the attacks on the gurdwaras. He tried to portray work as routine business, whereas it was anything but.

Various newspapers reported conflicting accounts of the incidents, and the death toll in Amritsar and other cities ranged from the mid-hundreds to the high thousands, but the details remained murky. Cities across Punjab struggled for many weeks to return to a normal life, and the future impact of the whole operation was incalculable. Such incidents don't just end there—there were always aftershocks.

Chetan's school had started, and school picked up right

where they had left off, as if nothing had happened. Teachers lacked the skills to discuss any topics of fear, violence, or killings with the children. They were going through their own fears, traumas, and anger. No family was untouched by the evil that surrounded them. Punishments at the school became more frequent and severe. So did the beatings at home. Any minor dereliction would lead to complaints at home, and Renu's punishments became more violent.

"Show me your test?" Renu demanded.

Chetan handed it to her. "Here."

"Why is there minus two from the total?"

"Because I got a black mark."

"What's a black mark?"

"When you are talking in class, the class monitor gives you a black mark, and then the teacher deducts two points." Chetan tried to choose his words carefully. Still, there was no way to make this sound better. The minus two was there in front of him.

Renu spewed fury. She lost all composure and control, and the weeks of pent-up anger and frustration exploded like a volcano hungry to taste blood. She removed her slipper, her weapon of choice, and rained blow after blow on Chetan's back.

"How dare you? After all the sacrifices I make for you . . . I walk to your school on foot, to the doctor on foot, and don't take a rickshaw . . . so that I can save some money and buy you fruits!"

With each sentence, the slipper would tear into Chetan's skin.

"And this is what you do at school? How dare you? *How dare you!*"

Chetan dropped to the floor. He was in a fetal position, his arms wrapped around his head, and his eyes closed."Mama, please! Mama, it hurts. Mama, sorry, I'll not do it again!"

But there was no escape from Renu's wrath. The slipper continued its barrage on his back and bottom.

Chetan was screaming. Tears were flowing nonstop. His nose was dripping. He was hyperventilating, losing his breath and his voice with every other word that came out of his mouth. He did not eat lunch that day and passed out on his bed. No one was to speak to him. Vikki stayed in his room. He knew to stay there till things settled down. Renu did not tell Vijay about the incident. Even if she did, Vijay would not care much. He was dealing with his fears and stress from the daily commute to the office. Renu did not ask Chetan to join the dinner table, and Vijay did not ask why.

Chetan went to sleep hungry.

His body ached terribly the following day. He could not lie on his back. He went to the bathroom to check his bruises—and it was black and blue. He lowered his shorts, looking back at his bottom. He could see a complete imprint of Renu's slipper, and tears fell down his cheek. He blamed himself for causing his mother such pain. The eleven-year-old asked God for forgiveness and promised to be a better son. He still loved his mother.

Chetan would change after that day. His charming smile and naughtiness were beaten out of him and replaced with even deeper cautiousness. He promised himself that this was the last time he would give his mother a chance to beat him. But unfortunately, the change came with a cost: his confidence, inner strength, and self-worth disappeared. He would never question any authority, and he would never talk back. Chetan worked hard at school; there were no black marks on his answer sheets and no complaints from the teachers again. He was more cautious in checking and rechecking his homework and his examination answer sheets. But he was sinking into a darker place. Any sudden noise would startle him, and he formed an annoying habit of looking behind his back frequently as if someone was continuously following him.

Tremors, sleepless nights, palpitations, and sweating became frequent. Chetan had no idea what an anxiety attack was. He did not learn about that term for another fifteen years. Still, he had to continuously endure it over the coming months and confront it for the rest of his life.

By constructing rituals, Chetan developed various coping mechanisms to deal with the continuous thoughts of imminent death and the unending fog of gloom. Say "Ram Ram" one hundred and eight times before sleeping; while walking, do not step over the lines on the floor; always put your shoes in straight lines; do not touch the lines on the floor; check if the door is closed, again, and again, and again. The rituals exhausted him, but those were the only things that gave him some sense of control. The practices brought him some sense of security, an armor that would save him from bad things. The strange logic kept taking deeper roots.

If I keep thinking about the horrible things, they will not happen. So, I must think of something going wrong.

And in any situation, Chetan was always thinking of the worst-case scenarios.

"If I take the bus, there will be a bomb blast.

If I eat outside, I will get sick and die.

If I do not submit the homework, I'll be expelled from school, and my parents will throw me out of the house.

If there is a stomach ache, it must be cancer.

His obsessive behavior took over. By thinking about these terrible things, he believed he could keep them from happening in real life. This became Chetan's daily, hourly struggle, always thinking of the worst-case scenario in everything in his life.

Punjab and its people were soiling in the ground. Broken, betrayed, bloodied, and tired from this never-ending struggle to stay alive with seemingly no end to their despair. For Chetan, the feeling of sadness became an intrinsic part of his being. He would not be able to shake this anxiety and fear out of his system for the rest of his life, no matter how hard he tried.

10

July 1984: Stepping Outside

By mid-July, the government had started to relax the night curfew in the cities. Life had not yet returned to normal, but people sought a sense of normalcy. The markets began opening until later in the evening, and factories ramped up production, making up for the lost time. Schools were closed for the summer holidays, and Chetan spent most of his time inside at home. His routine included waking up late, reading comic books or playing Ludo with Vikki, and occasionally venturing out in the evening to a nearby open plot of land for a game of cricket with neighborhood kids.

Sporadic news of killings still made the news, but less often. People tried to figure out whether they were moving toward peace or if the press was underreporting the incidents. The media seemed reluctant to report anything that might upset one community or the other.

Vijay was busy in his factory. His daily commute to the office now had new carpool partners. His friends did not want him to drive alone, and a couple volunteered to join him and form a new carpool. Renu busied herself with the kids at home. Phone lines were restored in Ferozepur, though phones remained a rarity for the Indian middle class. If someone wanted a new connection, the waiting line was several months. The lone service provider, the Department of Telecommunications, a state-run operator, was in no hurry to make services available to more citizens, and customer service was almost nonexistent. Renu and Vijay were lucky that his office provided the phone. She called her brother and her father almost daily. But calls on the phone did not make up for trips to her parents' home. She had not visited her parents in Ferozepur for a while now. She used to take the kids there every summer and was missing family more than usual. Events from the last months had drained her, and she wanted to take a break from all the housework, childcare, and constant worry.

Renu missed the support system she found at her parents' house. As such, one evening, when Vijay returned from work, she approached him and carefully brought up the subject.

"I was thinking about taking the kids to Ferozepur," she suggested. "Some change will be good for them. And, it is their vacation time." She looked at Vijay.

"You want to travel now?" Vijay said as he lowered his newspaper. Renu's fair complexion was pale, and her hair was messy from her afternoon nap. She had not kept her daily evening routine of combing and braiding her hair before Vijay came home.

"Yes, things seem calmer now." She mainly was trying to convince herself.

"Very well. Do you want to take the bus or train?" Vijay asked impassively.

Deep creases crinkled Renu's forehead. Her nose wrinkled,

lips twitched. Vijay's indifference infuriated her.

Does he not care about the family anymore? Vijay did not fight with her or try to stop her from going, and she hated him for that.

"I'll take the train. My brother will pick me up from the station," she replied in an icy tone.

"I'll get the tickets and drop you at the railway station this Saturday," Vijay said without deigning to lower the paper.

Renu boiled with rage. Vijay's avoidance of confrontation and his complete aversion to sharing his actual feelings kept them apart. Renu stormed from the room and into the kitchen.

Cooking was especially loud that evening. Utensils were striking each other hard as if they were in a proxy war. Running the tap, stirring, and kneading the dough—everything was extra loud. Renu and Vijay spoke little with each other for the next several days. And Chetan was aware of what was happening. He had learned to detect these situations and became extra careful lest he got the worst of his mother. Therefore, he kept his distance from her and avoided asking for anything while the situation between Renu and Vijay was still simmering. However, he was happy that they could finally venture out of the house and spend their summer vacation at their grandparents' home.

Chetan and Vikki were looking forward to visiting their little getaway. Their grandmother had passed away a few years back, and their grandfather was not very social. He was not the kind who would indulge in small talk with kids. He spent most of his day in his library with his vast collection of books and smoking Wills Navy Cut. However, Renu's brother and wife were very affectionate. Chetan and his brother often joined Mom, Mom's brother—Mama Ji, and his wife—Mami Ji, for evenings and nights of endless laughs, gossip, and occasionally a movie on the VCR.

Chetan could not wait for limitless access to the VCR. He had heard from his school friends about a new artist, Prince, who recently released a new album and a movie. *Purple Rain* was the talk among his friends. Unfortunately, Vijay and Renu did not care much for Hollywood movies, and there was no chance the film would run at local theaters in Patiala. Those theaters played only Hindi movies. Chetan could only see *Purple Rain* at his friend's place or at the home of one of his second cousins in Ferozepur. That's what he planned—a list of movies that he would watch while in Ferozepur, and *Purple Rain* was on top of the list. Many of those cousins studied in India's top boarding schools and returned home for the summer. They were more attuned to the Western world and news—news such as the fact that the first African-American Miss America, Vanessa Williams, had just been stripped of her crown when her nude photos were published in a magazine called *Penthouse*. Chetan had never heard of *Penthouse*, but he overheard some older kids at school giggling about the news.

The preparations for their trip to Ferozepur had begun. Vijay had booked the tickets for the eight-hour journey. It was peak summer, and traveling on the train without air-conditioning was not a pleasant experience. In addition, the apprehension of traveling during the period of unrest dampened the excitement. Thankfully, their trip would take place during the day, when chances of any kind of attack were minimal.

Renu began Chetan and Vikki's training again.

"Do not speak with anyone on the train. What are your names if someone asks you?" She rehearsed the Sikh pseudonyms for them, Kartar and Angad.

"And what do you say if someone asks why you cut your hair?" she asked again.

"Because we are coming from Delhi and cut our hair to be safe," Chetan replied.

This conversation made his legs tremble. Suddenly, the excitement of visiting Ferozepur turned into the fear of a dreaded journey he no longer wanted to take. A couple of steel *kadas* were bought from the gurdwara and put on Chetan's and Vikki's right wrists. The *kada* symbolized strength, but that day, it reminded Chetan of the danger that was always lurking around them.

The day of departure arrived, and Vijay loaded the luggage and kids in his green Fiat and drove them to the railway station. It was early in the morning, and the roads were empty. They were at the station within fifteen minutes. He bought his platform ticket, and they all went inside and waited on platform number 1 for the train's arrival. The railway station was unusually empty. Typically, a few hundred people milled about at the station at any time. During better days, the station used to be busy with dozens of hawkers selling tea, samosas, and kulche-chole. Their loud calls, accompanied by the aroma of freshly made hot food, added to the excitement of travel. Simply being on the platform used to be exciting in itself.

But not in 1984.

People avoided travel and most vendors had left the station due to a lack of travelers.

Chetan and Vikki were sitting on suitcases next to their parents. Vijay looked at Renu for a lengthy moment, as though questioning her decision to take the kids on a journey at this time. He did not say anything; he never did. He just shook his head, making his disapproval clear, and then looked away.

Renu avoided eye contact with him as well. She looked in the direction from which the train was to come.

Half an hour later, the train arrived, and Vijay helped lift the luggage and took the three of them to their seats inside the train. He slid the suitcases under the seat, waved bye to the kids, and left. Renu and he exchanged no words. They were not talking to each other. The tension between them was making Chetan more nervous about the trip. He was relieved as Vijay stepped out of their railcar and walked out of the station. Chetan directed his thoughts toward all the fun he would have at his grandparents' home. Station loudspeakers were blaring the departure announcements, and a few people were running along the platform to find their train car and board. Soon, the train horn made deafening sounds, and the train left the station. Chetan took the window seat. There was always a fight between him and his younger brother for the window seat, and Chetan won the argument on the grounds that the elder one gets to sit first, and then they would exchange seats after every train stop. Chetan looked outside the window as the train departed the city and soon ran beside the farming lands and fruit orchards.

The sun hit its peak, spewing scorching heat. The lack of air conditioning made for severe discomfort; however, the breeze from the open window kept the journey tolerable. The warm breeze blew through Chetan's hair as they made their way toward Ferozepur. Renu kept reminding him not to put his arm outside the window. There have been incidents of people losing their arms in moving train accidents. The warning only added to Chetan's heightened anxiety.

The train compartment was full. There were always more

109

people on the train than the seats. Many just sat on the floor, eating, chatting, or playing cards. Rummy was the game of choice. Chetan kept an eye on them.

Chetan was as vigilant as ever, as was Renu. He looked at everyone with suspicion, especially any newly boarded individual. Chetan grew increasingly uncomfortable among all these strangers. All bags seemed questionable to him, as if they were all hiding a bomb. Any person with loose clothing appeared to be hiding a gun. If anyone took out a knife to cut fruits, Chetan's imagination would run wild, fearing that person would start slitting throats at any moment.

Chetan considered various ways he could save himself if something happened. Should he pull the emergency chain and report the suspicious-looking person, run to a different train compartment, or just keep staring outside the window and avoid looking at them, so they would not pick him out in case a massacre started. He was tightly clasping his hands and praying, hoping to fall asleep and avoid all these thoughts. Soon, he dozed off and woke up just an hour before reaching Ferozepur. He slept for almost four hours. Chetan looked around, relieved that all was well and they were so close to home. He transitioned his mind again from uneasy to happy thoughts.

Soon, they arrived at Ferozepur.

The train stopped at the station, and Chetan's eyes scanned the platform, looking for his uncle, Mama Ji. He was there, waiting. As the train stopped, a servant leaped into the train, got their luggage down, hauled it out of the station into the parking lot, and tied everything on top of the parked car. Renu sat in the front seat with her brother, and the two kids sat in the back. The servant took his bicycle and rode back home.

He was not to sit in the car with them.

The melody of birdsong and the gentle rustle of leaves welcomed them as they drove toward their grandparents' home. The children were looking forward to spending their days exploring the village and indulging in delicious homemade meals cooked by their doting Mami Ji with the help of her cooks.

They reached home in twenty minutes. The sun was making its way down, and the air was getting cooler. They arrived home right at the time for the evening high tea. Hot samosas and jalebi were ready, and the cook was asked to make the tea. Chetan's mouth was watering at the sight of alluring, crisp fried samosas. He was looking at that plate on the coffee table at the center of the large drawing room. Stifling his urge to gobble it all up, Chetan walked straight to his grandfather, who sat on his sofa. The kids approached him cautiously and touched his feet for a blessing. Renu bowed her head in front of him. With the slightest smile, he put his hand on everyone's head, one at a time. No one expected any more emotion from him than that.

"Is everything going well at home?" he asked.

"Yes, Papa," Renu replied.

"Is Vijay doing fine?"

"Yes."

"Is his work going well?"

"Yes."

"Good."

Following this brief catch-up, he sipped his tea and continued reading his book.

Renu asked the kids if they wanted milk or tea. Chetan took tea and Vikki milk. Chetan always preferred drinking tea—

111

the taste of milk nauseated him. Soon, Renu, her brother, and his wife got busy with their gossip, and Vikki and Chetan ran outside to the huge brick-layered front yard and set it up for a game of cricket.

The following day, Chetan and Vikki woke up early. During visits to their grandparents' house, Chetan and Vikki began their mornings by accompanying the servants to get fresh milk from the two cows that were raised at home. They then fed the cows and joined the cooks in the kitchen to churn the curd and cream from the day before to make butter and buttermilk. They had so much buttermilk that they had to give it away daily. People from the nearby village would know that Chetan's grandparents' house always had extra and lined up outside the house in the morning to get some. The servants kept some for the family and distributed the rest to the people waiting outside.

Soon, the breakfast was ready. One of the servants called everyone to the dining room, where Chetan's grandfather sat at the head of the table. He was always served first. Chetan asked for his favorite, fried eggs and toast with fresh butter from that day. There was no better taste for Chetan than the taste of sweet, freshly churned butter over the dark, crunchy, warm toast. Chetan hastily munched on the toast with a thick layer of butter and a fried egg stacked on top. He did not want to miss the tractor ride. Every day, a worker from the farm came to their house to pick up the tractor. The tractor was always parked in the vast open yard in front of the house. He picked up the tractor every morning, took it to the farm, and returned it in the evening. Chetan and Vikki awaited his arrival.

"Namaste, Ram Lal Ji," Chetan called from far away as soon

as he saw the farm worker entering the main gate. "Can you take us around the park?"

Ram Lal happily agreed. There was a huge smile on his face, partially hidden under his big handlebar mustache. He picked them up one by one and seated them on the tractor, then took them for a quick ride around the park in front of the house. The rhythmic hum of the tractor's engine blended with the giggles of Chetan and Vikki; their eyes sparkled with unbridled delight. Chetan felt free and happy, away from all worries.

Once back home, Chetan ran up to the terrace of their bungalow and sat down on the wooden cot weaved with jute ropes. He was at peace, reading his comic book and occasionally looking at the kites flying in the sky. He was looking out for any kite fight that would lead to a losing kite falling onto his terrace. Chetan had found a happy place.

Lunch often included chicken or mutton curry, rare delicacies in Chetan's home. Although Vijay was a vegetarian, he never prohibited Renu from cooking or eating meat. She would generally cook it for lunch while Vijay was in the office or when he was traveling for work.

Chetan was in and out of the kitchen, waiting for the special mutton curry to be ready. The aroma of spices fried in the homemade ghee was overpowering. The cook was adding onions, tomatoes, and then meat, all from their farm. Chetan watched him intently, noticing how the smell of fried spices changed to the sweet smell of cooked onion and then to tangy when tomatoes were added. The other cook was outside, firing the tandoor in the backyard. Chetan joined him and helped out by adding the dried straws and wood to the fire as he got the clay oven ready for tandoori rotis. The lunch included a

113

variety of fresh tandoori rotis stuffed with onions, mashed potatoes, or green chickpeas.

The whole family gathered in the dining room again for lunch. Chetan feasted on mutton and tandoori rotis, dripping with homemade butter and a glass of chilled lassi from that day's fresh buttermilk. Lunch was followed by an afternoon siesta by the adults. Chetan and Vikki sneaked back to the terrace to read comic books and play with an old set of Mechano, Chetan's favorite toy. Chetan and Vikki were clearly instructed by Renu not to disturb her afternoon nap.

She wanted to make the best of her break as well.

11

August 1984: The Dark One

The days at their grandparents' house seemed to blend into each other. Chetan and Vikki continued their morning routines of cow feeding, butter churning, and tractor rides. Once a day, Renu would remind the kids to do their summer homework. Chetan was to finish reading an abridged version of *David Copperfield* and write a summary. He had not read even half of the book, and his anxiety over missing a deadline began to set in. He did not want to return to the school without the required ten-page book summary.

Chetan did not enjoy reading novels, unlike his grandfather, who spent his whole day reading in his library. Chetan considered asking him for some assistance but was too scared of him to ask for any help. His grandfather did not have much of a close relationship with his grandchildren, and conversations between them were very cursory.

Chetan and Vikki spent their days at various cousins' places, watching movies, playing cricket, or occasionally visiting the family farm, and watching the 1984 Summer Olympics highlights on the TV, where India was not doing very well. Still, there were hopes of bringing back the field hockey gold.

The 1984 Summer Olympics were marred with controversy yet again. The city of Los Angeles was the host, and the cold war was still on. Following the US boycott of the 1980 Olympics in Moscow, the Soviet Union returned the favor. The USSR and many Eastern Bloc allies boycotted the Olympics. Although India had close relations with the USSR, India considered itself a nonaligned country. India, the pioneer of the Non-Aligned Movement (NAM), sent forty-eight athletes to participate in the 1984 Summer Olympics Games. In retrospect, India should have stayed out of the games. It was one of India's worst performances at the games, and the athletes returned without any medals. The only silver lining was P. T. Usha, who came fourth in the four-hundred-meter hurdles and got a hero's welcome on his return. The celebrated Indian field hockey team did not reach the semifinals.

To rub salt in the wound, Pakistan, India's archrival, won the field hockey gold. Everyone attributed this to the USA's support for Pakistan and them getting favorable conditions. On the other hand, India, being friends with the USSR, was given the worst pairings and got eliminated. Conspiracy theories to justify the losses. Chetan did not buy into those. He was captivated by the strength and dominance of the US athletes—they exhibited strength, confidence, and skill. They played to win. They came to every arena with such high spirits and with a determination that crushed opponents' morale. Chetan dreamed of such self-confidence and grit and admired those athletes. But, of course, many attributed the US dominance in the games to the absence of the USSR. Chetan hoped he would one day visit the United States of America and watch the Olympics live there.

For now, Chetan enjoyed spending time at various cousins' homes, but being with those cousins made him more aware of things he did not have. They were fair-skinned, green-eyed kids, just like Renu. People used to say that Chetan looked like his mother, but unfortunately, he did not get her fair skin or her green eyes. On top of it, those kids were rich. They had access to every possible comfort, such as VCRs, air conditioners, Nike and Gola shoes, and Levi's jeans—all foreign brands, many of which Chetan had never heard of. As much as he enjoyed their company, a part of him felt uncomfortable with their affluence.

Chetan looked to Mom's support to overcome his insecurities, but she always made him feel worse. Visiting the homes of other Ferozepur relatives with Renu brought him anxiety. Chetan was darker than any of Renu's relatives' children, and she was embarrassed about bringing an ugly brown duckling to her relatives' place. One afternoon, Chetan overheard Renu say to her brother, "I am so embarrassed when I see this kid sitting among all the other children. They all are fair and pretty, and mine is dark and ugly." She followed up her hateful but casual comment with a loud bark of laughter. Her brother, however, was not amused.

"Looking good is not everything. Many of those pretty kids are failing in school." Chetan's uncle pushed back.

Chetan stood behind the door, away from Renu's eyes, his head hanging low. He was frozen and did not know whether to go and ask Renu for what he had come to ask for or just to walk away. Renu's words had pierced Chetan's heart. Still, he tried to brush off her comments and convince himself that

117

his mother's words were in jest. He wanted to believe that his mother would never be so cruel. However, there was a lingering question of whether she had unconditional love for him. How could a mother find her own son to be ugly? She was his mother, and he tried everything to make her happy and proud. He did not approach Renu, took a few steps back, away from the room, and ran to the rooftop. Chetan never forgot his mother's embarrassment for him and kept trying to win her love and affection.

Chetan became accustomed to scorn and had learned to pull himself up. He continued playing with his fair-skinned cousins. After all, they had everything that Chetan lacked in his home back in Patiala. Sometimes, Chetan would bring up studies or ask them how many marks they got in their last exams to show that he had some edge over them, too. Most of the cousins were barely passing their classes. It was not uncommon for them to spend more than a year in a class. They were not under any pressure to study hard, as their parents knew that the kids would all end up managing the family farms or other businesses. Chetan and Vikki were a couple of grades ahead of their cousins of the same age, and that made Chetan feel good.

Their time at Ferozepur was coming to an end. There were just a couple of days left before their train journey back. Chetan's school was to start the following week, and the *David Copperfield* summary was not yet complete. Chetan asked for his mother's help. She passed the job to her brother, who promised to help but forgot. Chetan tried his best to read the book but could not go beyond the first three chapters.

Why did the teacher have to ruin the summer holiday with such an assignment?

118

Preparations for travel back home had started. Renu visited tailors to get her new *salwar* suits back. As she was the daughter of the house, her parents bought her new clothes every time she visited. It was a tradition not to send her back home without gifts. And Renu's father took that tradition seriously. In the past, Renu's mother took her shopping. Now, Renu's father asked her brother to give Renu money so that she could go to the bazaar with her sister-in-law to do the shopping. The outing also included buying shirts and shorts for the kids and a toy or two. Chetan and Vikki spent the last few evenings accompanying Renu to fabric stores to buy cloth and then to tailors for measurements and stitching. As soon as the sun's heat got tolerable, they would leave the house to Gali No. 12 market, where Renu scanned through various shops and, in between, stopped for a food break at chaat vendors lined up along the street.

Mami Ji, Chetan's aunt, had instructed the cooks to prepare pickles for Renu to take back home. In winter, they made pickles with carrots, cauliflower, and turnips. And, in the summer, it was mangoes, a special fali—beanstalks, and green wild berries were used to make the pickle in mustard oil. Renu also ordered some wheat flour and desi ghee biscuits at a local bakery. Chetan's grandfather instructed Ram Lal, the farm worker, to bring back a sack of wheat and onion from the farm storage when he returned to drop the tractor in the evening.

Bringing all the gifts back from her parent's house filled Renu with pride. It was a way for her to show Vijay that she belonged to a wealthy family and had a support system beyond him. On her return, she never failed to tell her neighbors in Patiala all the stuff she got back from her *maika*, her maternal home. Receiving all this stuff from his in-laws irritated Vijay and, deep down, hurt his ego. But he never said anything to Renu. As usual, he avoided confrontation.

The day of the return train journey had arrived. Chetan's uncle had bought the tickets, and servants packed food and water for the trip. The car was loaded with the luggage, and a carrier was attached to the roof to hold the sacks of wheat and onions. Chetan said his goodbyes by touching his grandfather's feet and giving Mami Ji a big hug. It was hard for Chetan to leave, and he dragged his feet and sat in the front of the car, next to the driver's seat. They arrived at the railway station quickly; too soon for Chetan. Mama Ji called a coolie to take the luggage from the car to the platform. The train was there within fifteen minutes. All goods were loaded onto the train, Chetan, Renu, and Vikki took their seats, and the return journey started.

The travel back felt longer. The anticipation of all the fun was now replaced by the dread of school and home chores. Chetan's face was gloomy. He remained quiet. He looked at Renu, who was silent as well. Her eyes were still moist with tears. She was looking out of the window.

Why is Mama crying? Is she missing Nana's home? Does she not want to go back?

All kinds of thoughts were running through Chetan's head. He became more anxious about the book report with each passing station. And, the train ride during the time of political turmoil added to his anxiety.

Chetan was back on high alert, watching every person on the train. He again scrutinized every moving passenger, every bag they carried, and every blanket they wrapped around themselves, wondering if there could be any hidden bomb or a gun. Chetan was again clasping his hands, trying to force his mind to think about something else. He tried to pray and think about some good times, but nothing was helping.

The train traveled at a good pace till it stopped at the Bathinda station, halfway from Ferozepur to Patiala. The train was held there for more than two hours. Bathinda was a big railway junction where the train cars changed lines and were added to engines for different destinations, a procedure called shunting. Some passengers on the train started asking why the shunting was taking so long.

Shunting, what a funny-sounding word, Chetan thought.

That day, it was taking longer than usual. Typically, that stop was for forty-five minutes, giving people some time to get off the train and buy meals or snacks. Such a long wait had people talking in subdued voices. Many feared the worst.

"Is there another train attack somewhere?"

"Is the train being held by some protests?"

"Is there going to be an attack on this train?"

The noise of crying babies and sobbing elderly women became more ominous. The situation grew grimmer with every passing minute. Patiala was still three hours away. Renu's eyes were getting moist again. This fear exacerbated her sadness about leaving her parents' home. She clutched Vikki hard by her side, while Chetan occupied the seat in front of her, staring blankly at her. He wanted to be close to her. He wanted to say something to her, to pacify her, but he did not know how to have that conversation. He went back to his praying, saying, "Ram, Ram, Ram . . ." one hundred and eight times, again and again.

The train eventually started to move and picked up speed. The guard came to their car and told everyone that there had been some mechanical breakdown in the engine, and they were

121

all set to reach the Patiala station in four hours.

Upon arriving, Chetan scanned the platform as the train entered the Patiala station. Vijay awaited them. Chetan waved at him vigorously with his hands outside the window. As the train halted, Vijay walked toward their carriage and jumped into it. There was a smile on his face. Chetan and Vikki were happy to see him. They leaped into his arms, giving him a big hug.

Renu had a smile on her face as well. They both seemed to be relieved to see each other safe. Vijay called the coolie to take the baggage and big sacks of wheat and onion from the train to his car. Vijay did not seem annoyed with all that stuff. Chetan was happy to see both his parents excited and smiling. They quickly loaded the car and drove toward home.

Chetan always loved the smell of home when they came back from vacations. It smelled sweet, their own. The rosy scent from the incense stick that Vijay lighted every day for his prayers, a scent that lingered throughout the day. Chetan's bed was waiting for him. His collection of comic books was there, to which he would add what he bought from Ferozepur. He now had 133. The family soon gathered for dinner, and the TV was on. Renu did not have to cook that evening. The landlady, Mrs. Randhawa, had sent two subzis and some rotis. She was a generous lady who always sent food whenever the family returned from travel.

Chetan was eager to try out the new pickle they had brought home. Renu reminded him that it needed a few more days to be good, but Chetan was not ready to wait. It was Vijay's favorite pickle too, so he went ahead and opened it. Soon after dinner, Renu made some tea, and the kids went off to their rooms.

Chetan was staring at the ceiling. The book report still needed to be done, and school was in a few days. The feeling of fear got more potent with each passing minute. Lights were out for all rooms, but Chetan's eyes were still wide open. Overwhelmed with fear and emotion, Chetan had a sudden outburst. He began to cry. So hard and loud that Vijay came over to his room and asked what was happening.

"I have a book report due on Monday," Chetan said between sobbing, confessing his turmoil about the elusive assignment.

"What report?" Vijay asked without anger.

"I had to read *David Copperfield* and write a summary."

"I read that book during my school."

"Have you?"

"Yes, that and *Oliver Twist*."

"Can you help me with that?"

"Yes, we can start on Saturday and finish by Sunday evening."

Chetan found a lifeline, a promise of shared understanding and the relief of not facing the challenge alone. The weight on his shoulders lifted, replaced by the warmth of his dad's support that he always craved. Chetan went to sleep happy.

The following day, Vijay woke him up, and they started reading through the book chapters. After each chapter, Vijay wrote notes, and Chetan copied them in his English notebook. Chetan admired Vijay's handwriting and always wanted to emulate it. He enjoyed this time with his Dad, one of the few times he did schoolwork with his father. Together, they completed the report by 11:00 p.m. on Sunday.

Chetan woke up Monday morning confident, looking forward to showcasing his book report in class.

"I bet most of the students would not have done it!"

Today would be the day to impress the English teacher, Ms.

Sharma.

And maybe, somehow, his mother.

12

September 1984: The Uproar

Chetan returned to school excited to meet his friends after a gap of two months. There was so much to talk about. He was curious about what others did during their holidays. Where did they go? What movies did they watch? Which restaurants did they eat at? He was curious about new toys or sports items anyone bought during the holidays. If anyone had bought a new cricket bat or a basketball, they brought it to the school on the first day. Those were things to show off during the playtime before school started and during recess.

Chetan got up early for the first day of school. He eagerly put on his school uniform—white shirt, light blue pants, a tie of the same color, and well-polished black shoes—and hurriedly finished his breakfast. His backpack was ready the previous night, and he had double-checked that he had the notebook with the book summary. He said bye to Renu, picked up his bag, and left for school on his bicycle. That was the advantage of going to school on his own bike. He did not have to wait for the rickshaw like Vikki did. He wanted to get to school early.

If he got to school early enough, before the assembly bell rang, he could spend the time on the playground catching up with his friends. Chetan reached the school at 7:40 a.m., dropped his bag on his assigned desk in the class, and ran toward the playground.

School started at 8:00 a.m. sharp, with the peon ringing the school bell. All grades lined up for the morning assembly. Chetan took his place in the line for his sixth-grade section B.

The assembly began with the prayer, "Our Father in heaven, hallowed be your name . . ." Chetan and Vikki went to a Catholic school that was established in the 1960s and run by Catholic nuns. Students from all religious and economic backgrounds attended. Still, many city residents felt that the school had a hidden agenda to influence and convert children to Christianity. Considered one of the best schools in Patiala, it was highly regarded for its academics, and Vijay had to pull many strings to get Chetan and Vikki admitted to this school. The prayer was followed by PT– five minutes of morning exercises – and then the principal welcomed everyone back. As the morning assembly concluded, the PT teacher directed everyone to go to their rooms in single-file lines, one class at a time. By 8:30 a.m., everyone had taken a seat at their desks.

Chetan was in his class, sitting at his desk and eagerly waiting for the English teacher, Ms. Sharma, to ask about the assignment. As Ms. Sharma entered the class, the kids shouted in unison, "Good Morning, ma'am!"

"Please put your holiday homework on the table," Ms. Sharma instructed.

"Who has not completed the book summary?" she asked.

About a dozen kids, out of forty-two, slowly and hesitantly raised their hands. Chetan knew what was in store for them.

He turned his head and scanned all the kids with their hands in the air. He could see fear in their eyes. Ms. Sharma was not one to let it go lightly. He expected her to send them to the principal's office, have them stand outside the class with their hands up for the rest of the period, or give the usual punishment of hitting their knuckles with a wooden ruler. The class had a pin-drop silence, and everyone wondered what would happen next.

"You all have a week to finish and submit."

There was an audible sigh of relief from the kids with their hands raised. A little sheepish smile was coming back on their faces. Disappointment flooded Chetan. All that anxiety and stress he'd carried with him for the last two months—for nothing. There were no consequences for anyone who did not complete their work. It did not seem fair. He quietly approached the teacher's table and placed his notebook on the stack. He briefly looked into Ms. Sharma's eyes, as if asking why she was letting them off easy. After all, she was one of the strictest teachers in the school. Maybe the circumstances had softened her. Perhaps she did not want to inflict pain on the children in addition to what they were already going through. This was a new side of her that Chetan had never seen. Strangely and despite everything, it comforted him.

September was already here, and Chetan's school classes were in full force. MTV was hot on the scene, and everyone in the school talked about it. MTV was going to hold its first Video Music Awards on September 14. Cable TV was not yet available in Patiala, but the Doordarshan channel sometimes broadcasted some recordings late at night. Madonna and Michael Jackson were all the rage at school, and the kids had all the songs memorized. Many of Chetan's friends had

Madonna and *Thriller* posters on their walls. Chetan was thinking about getting a poster, too. Maybe Michael Jackson's, but he wondered how his father would react if he even asked. Vijay was not open to many conversations unless they were about studies. Any discussion outside that was considered a waste of time. He insisted that Chetan and Vikki should focus only on their education. He always reminded them that they needed to prioritize education to become something worthwhile when they grew up. It would ruin their lives if they did not study hard and failed to get into a good college to become an engineer or a doctor. Vijay had experienced a hard life after the death of his father. He knew how hard it was for his mother to run the household, and he understood that education was his only ticket to pull himself away from the edges of poverty. Vijay feared that if his sons did not stay focused on their studies, they would have no future. He did not relate much to art, music, or pop-culture ideas, and did not encourage any such discussions at home.

Chetan was sitting beside his dad as he was having his evening tea, reading the newspaper, and listening to the TV news, all at the same time. Chetan was looking for an opportunity to talk about the poster. He sat still, hands clasped between his knees and rocking back and forth as if to gain momentum before a launch. The evening news on TV announced the birth of Prince Harry, the second son of Prince Charles and Lady Diana. It was covered in the newspaper as well. Chetan's thoughts vacillated between the poster and all the rumors about the royal couple's rocky relationship.

"Papa?"

"Yes."

"Can I—" Chetan cut himself off.

128

"Do you need any books? Pens?" Vijay asked.

Are books or stationery the only things that one could need? Chetan thought. At that moment, asking Vijay for money to buy a poster did not sound like a good idea.

"No. It's nothing." He stood and walked to his room, thinking maybe he could bring it up later if he scored good marks on the midterm exams.

But things remained stressful around the house. There was never a good time.

He did not bring up the conversation again.

It was more than three months since the Indian army had taken over Punjab. The wounds of the attack on gurdwaras were still fresh. There were no signs of them healing anytime soon. The army's extended presence in Punjab turned people against the current regime and the prime minister, Indira Gandhi. People felt that the government had turned a blind eye to people's woes. Business was down, people were struggling, and the government was busy preparing for the upcoming elections.

Even the moderate citizens were now getting tired of the army's presence in their cities. They were becoming increasingly dissatisfied with the central government's management of the situation in Punjab. The government was considered inept in understanding and handling the situation. Intellectuals and other moderates across the state were showing their dissent. The uproar against the government was most vocal in Amritsar, and the waves of dissent started reaching Patiala and all other corners of the state.

Media and foreign journalists were still not allowed to cover the incidents in the state freely, and the national TV news channels seldom covered the ground reality. There was

129

an army presence in all major cities and villages bordering Pakistan. Military trucks patrolled the cities regularly. In many colleges and universities, parts of the campus were taken and converted into army residential units. The working class headed back to their offices, trying to get some sense of normality, but the youth, the college-going students, raised their voices and started showing less reverence for the military presence. The incidents of students picking altercations with soldiers manning road checkpoints were on the rise. The complete mistrust in the government's intentions and ongoing police brutalities fueled the undercurrents of rebellion.

Since the media was primarily inactive across the state, wild stories of conflicts between people and the army cropped up daily. There were talks about soldiers mercilessly beating students and students beating up a soldier in retaliation.

As citizens gathered back their courage and started to stand up against the army, incidents of public protest began to increase. Most of the time, protests ended without any incident. One morning, a college student union called for the closure of schools across the city to protest against police brutality. They went to schools and colleges across the city and forced the administration to close them down. Chetan was standing in his class line during the morning assembly when they stormed into Chetan's school, jumping over the walls, and forcing the gate open. They were carrying field hockey sticks, iron rods, and swords, and were screaming and shouting slogans on the top of their voices.

"Stop police violence!"

"Indian army, leave Punjab!"

"No peace till the army leaves!"

"Inquilab zindabad!"

130

The incident shook the students, and many started sobbing. Chetan stood there trembling with fear. The rage in their voices, the vitriol in their eyes, and the manic swinging of swords raised Chetan's heartbeat as he witnessed utter chaos unfurling in front of his eyes. He was trying his best not to cry in front of his classmates. A few union members ran into the principal's office, demanding an immediate school closure.

The school principal quickly obliged and announced that the school was closed for the day, and the parents were informed. The principal, a Catholic nun, did not see any point in taking the risk of confronting the attackers, who, although they represented the student union, seemed too old to be students. They were the next generation of politicians in the making, and this was their training ground.

Chetan walked toward his class hastily to collect his school-bag. Even though the unexpected school closure could have been a welcome surprise, today was very different. He had to summon all his courage to walk past the dozens of protesters shouting angrily outside the school and pick up his bicycle from the stand. Many parents came to get their children from school, but Chetan had to ride his bicycle back home. Vijay was in the office. Renu did not drive, and the only way she could reach the school was by a rickshaw. That would take too much time. Chetan rushed to Vikki's class and picked him up. Among the chaos of parents scrambling to find their kids and whisk them away on their scooters or in the cars, Chetan unlocked his bicycle from the stand and, rather than coming out of the main gate, he left from the small gate at the back of the school playground. Vikki rode pillion behind him. Chetan avoided the main road and rode his bike through the back allies of the neighborhoods to get back home. Those rides were the hardest ones. He constantly looked behind him, sometimes stopping by to look around the corner of the streets to see if there were any protesters. His goal was to avoid them at any cost and get home safely.

Rumors of army hostility spread. Talks about looting, rape, and killings by the army surfaced occasionally, although none of these were ever confirmed by the media or any government officials. There were allegations about the army locking people up and torturing them, raiding homes, and stealing from them. People accused the army of forcing them to sign false confession documents. One day, a certain group would make accusations against the army; the next day, another group would launch a protest to deny any wrongdoing by the army.

Vijay believed the army's presence would bring peace and maintain order. Withdrawal would lead to immediate chaos in the state. Thanks to the army, citizens could conduct their business, go to work, and return home safely.

The communities were divided about their acceptance of the army's presence. Some communities would welcome the soldiers as heroes, while others treated soldiers with hostility. Some shops and restaurants refused service to soldiers. Occasionally, servicemen were taunted as they patrolled neighborhoods. The army found itself in unchartered territory. Soldiers never had to deal with such extreme domestic unrest. They were not trained for it. They were not used to such hostility from their fellow citizens, especially in Punjab, where people held soldiers in high esteem.

Punjabi Sikhs had a long and proud history of serving in the Indian army. Punjabi units made up a significant portion of the army's strength. The martial traditions of the Punjabi people date back centuries, with the region producing some of the finest warriors on the subcontinent. During the colonial period, Punjabi soldiers played a vital role in the British Indian army, serving in various regiments and seeing action in numerous conflicts worldwide. Many legendary Indian army generals came from Punjab. In Punjab, joining the Indian army was one of the biggest dreams of many young boys. Some families had been sending their sons to the military for generations.

As Punjab was near the Pakistan border, many wars were fought on the land, and the army always had complete support from locals. People would feed soldiers and give them a place to stay warm at night. But, after the attacks on gurdwaras, things changed. The same people who held the army in the highest regard closed their doors on them. The hero soldier had become the villain. People did not trust the military anymore. All soldiers represented the desecration of the holy Golden Temple.

Presence in Punjab and policing the citizens had become uncomfortable for the army, and servicemen were out of their element and wanted an immediate exit. This was different from what they had been trained for. Fighting a foreign enemy was one thing, but fighting with citizens and losing respect was something they were unwilling to accept. The land that had held them in the highest regard was treating them as unwanted.

These were the times when it was complicated to discern fact from fiction. It was a period of fear, anger, confusion, and distress. And Chetan and his family were not immune to it. Chetan was the one worst affected by this constant anxiety, and the trip to school and back became laborious with each passing day. He was troubled by the news that was constantly filled with the coverage of violence.

133

After a short pause, killings on buses started again. So, too, did the explosions in major cities.

There was increasing pressure from citizens to get the army out of the state and bring the elected government back. Many blamed the central government for not listening to the people and establishing an unjust rule in the state. Fear spread that the army's stay would continue in Punjab because of the upcoming elections. However, people were not willing to wait that long. The army presence was considered a roadblock to any peace discussion between local leaders and the central government. Many senior state politicians were jailed, so they could not mobilize people for protests. Nonetheless, demonstrations happened organically.

The pressure on the central government increased, and they announced a phased army pullout to appease locals. The army started vacating the premises of the Golden Temple, and the news was celebrated across the state as a win against the central government. The government extended another olive branch by announcing monetary compensation to the families of civilians killed during the military operation. They were keen on diffusing the volatile situation. They planned to release many political detainees from prisons, expecting that these concessions could bring some peace back and help them with a favorable election outcome. The army was removed from the temple, and the restoration work began. Some politicians visited the temple to witness the progress and to inform the press that the work was being carried out as promised. The news was welcomed by many, but others continued to be skeptical. As the word of the army withdrawal reached the masses, the hope of peace emerged. People, once again, started to visit local temples and gurdwaras and prayed for peace.

Chetan and his family remained apprehensive and cautious. Life seemed to continue among the chaos of celebrations, protests, calls for school closures, and curfews. The schools were almost getting back to full sessions. Homework assignments and midterm exams kept Chetan busy. Most of his time was now spent inside the four walls of the house boundary. He seldom went out to his friend's place, and playing cricket on an empty lot of land was a thing of the past. Going to school and back was the only risk anyone was willing to take. Beyond that, keeping your head down and being inside homes was the norm. Laughter and enjoyment proved evasive. Life was stuck in a never-ending twilight zone of gloom.

13

October 1984: The Tree Fell

October 1984 brought such a vicious storm that it shook the nation to its core. The storm ripped people from their homes and uprooted them from their foundational values and beliefs.

Despite the army's removal from the Golden Temple and repeated assurances of complete army withdrawal from the state, there was a strong dissent against the ruling government, especially against the prime minister, Indira Gandhi. It was she who had ordered the Indian army to take over the Golden Temple in June 1984 to force insurgents out of the complex.

Indira Priyadarshini Gandhi, considered one of the most powerful women of the twentieth century, was the only child of Jawahar Lal Nehru, India's first prime minister. She had a first-row seat to Indian politics and was trained by the best statesmen of the time. Contrary to the prevalent trends for women in those times, no one confined her indoors or restricted her movement. She found herself in the midst of the good, the bad, and the ugly of politics. She came to power as the prime minister of India in 1966 after the death of her predecessor, Lal Bahadur Shastri. Many considered her the Iron Lady of India. There was a lot in common between her and the British prime minister Margret Thatcher, the Iron Lady. They were both the first female leaders of their democracies. Although they seldom agreed on politics and policies, they connected well personally. Both understood each other's struggles and the loneliness of being in the top position, especially if you were a woman. When Thatcher survived an assassination attempt on October 12, 1984, by the Irish Republican Army, Indira was one of the first to send her a message inquiring about her well-being. Thatcher would soon have an opportunity to reciprocate, but Gandhi's outcome differed.

Lal Bahadur Shastri succeeded Jawahar Lal Nehru, Indira's father, as the prime minister upon Nehru's death in 1964. Shastri supported Indira and gave her a seat in the Rajya Sabha, the upper house of the Indian parliament. On Shastri's sudden death in January 1966, Gandhi defeated Morarji Desai to become the party leader and succeeded Shastri as the prime minister. She won the support of many leaders who hoped that she would be a weak premier and they could easily control her as a puppet prime minister. She turned out to be anything but a puppet.

Rabindranath Tagore added Priyadarshini to her name— Indira Priyadarshini Gandhi. Priyadarshini means "looking at everything with kindness." A moniker history would debate.

Gandhi was ruthless with her policies and ruled with an iron fist. Indira shattered all the beliefs that she'd be a token leader who would be timid and could be manipulated politically. From a war with Pakistan that created Bangladesh to declaring an unpopular state of emergency in the seventies, she was known for exercising absolute control and political intransigence. But sending the army to the Golden Temple in Punjab and starting a war within India was beyond what anyone anticipated.

In 1977, after an extended period of emergency where she suspended all democratic processes, Indira Gandhi finally called elections to allow the electorate to vindicate her from the allegations of electoral manipulations. Unfortunately, she grossly misjudged her popularity and embarrassingly lost her seat and the elections, paving the way for Morarji Desai to become the next prime minister. Desai's government suffered instability, and the Congress Party under Gandhi was swept back into power in January 1980.

The situation in Punjab in the eighties was getting out of control for Indira Gandhi. The violence kept escalating, and the pressure on her government to get to a resolution kept increasing. She had been trying negotiations for a while, but no progress was made. However, she was not one to back out. In June 1984, Gandhi ordered the Indian army to enter the Golden Temple to remove separatist leaders and their supporters from the complex. The army was in unchartered waters, and so was Indira. It brought heavy artillery and tanks for the operation code-named Operation Blue Star. The operation was not an empty threat; it was a domestic war. The Golden Temple was severely damaged, with many parts destroyed. It led to the deaths of many separatists sheltered inside the Golden Temple and of innocent pilgrims who, unfortunately, were at the wrong place at the wrong time. The number of casualties, by some estimates, ran into the thousands.

Many blamed Gandhi for orchestrating and timing the

attack on the temple for political gains. The opposition alleged that she attacked the temple to portray herself as a hero and gain an advantage in the upcoming general elections. The criticism of her action was gaining momentum in India and overseas. Many Sikh organizations called for revenge. There were incidents of Sikh soldiers leaving the Indian army, Sikh leaders resigning from their administrative offices, and many notable public figures returning awards they'd received from the Indian government to protest the attack.

And then the unthinkable happened.

At 9:30 a.m. on October 31, 1984, Indira Gandhi was on her way to an interview with British filmmaker Peter Ustinov for an Irish television documentary. As she walked past a wicket gate, her own Sikh bodyguards shot her with their official firearms in the garden of the prime minister's residence at 1 Safdarjung Road, New Delhi, to avenge Operation Blue Star.

One bodyguard, Beant Singh, shot her three times in the abdomen. Beant Singh was one of her favorite guards; she had known him for many years. He was taken off her staff after Operation Blue Star because he was a Sikh. However, Indira had him reinstated. The other bodyguard shot her another thirty times using his submachine gun. She was taken to the hospital, where the doctors removed the bullets, but no one could survive such an attack—not even the Iron Lady of India, Indira Gandhi.

She was declared dead at 2:20 p.m.

The news of her assassination spread like wildfire.

As soon as school was over, Chetan rushed home. He rode his bicycle through the famous 22 No. Phatak market in Patiala that was bustling with activity. Many people gathered there, playing *dhols*–the drums, and dancing in celebration of the

139

death of Indira Gandhi. People were lining up outside the sweet shops to buy laddoos. The noise of fireworks was only getting stronger.

All this celebration of death made Chetan uneasy and scared. He kept his eyes straight on the road, trying not to make any eye contact with the people, and pedaled faster. As soon as Chetan made it home, he rushed to the TV. A teary newscaster on *Doordarshan*, Salma Sultan, gave the country the news of the assassination. The whole country fell into mourning, but the mood in Punjab differed. The noise of fireworks accompanied celebrations. Chetan was confused to witness such a strange juxtaposition of fear, sorrow, and celebration. He was not sure which side to support and whether to mourn or join the festivities. He felt neither sad nor happy. The only feeling he had was immense fear. If the country's prime minister could be killed by her own bodyguards, then who could be safe?

Chetan did not want to be alone and came outside, where people in the neighborhood were gathering among the loud noises of fireworks. Stoic, Renu stood beside the landlady, who was in a jubilant mood as she openly expressed her joy.

"Today, our hearts are at peace. The tyrant is dead," she said as Renu listened silently. Renu was not foolish enough to argue. Chetan looked at his mom for any cues on how to direct his emotions. He received none.

"Today, we all are going to dance the bhangra," the landlady said, overjoyed, "but after we visit the gurdwara. We have taken revenge for the insult to our religion." She was beyond herself.

The situation was similar at Vijay's office. As the news reached the office, some people were openly celebrating, and others were scared. Vijay was getting uncomfortable and

140

wanted to leave for home as soon as possible. He promptly left the office at five in the evening. On his way back home, he stopped by the vegetable vendor. In the morning, Renu had asked him to buy some mushrooms on his way back. Unfortunately, the street vendor who came to the home did not carry mushrooms. After dropping off his carpool colleagues, he stopped by a shop.

"How much are these?" Vijay asked the shopkeeper.

"You can take it for free today! I am so happy; my heart is full of joy," the vegetable store owner responded.

Vijay did not know how to react.

"Maybe later," he returned the mushroom pack and left the shop quickly, rushing toward the car. There was some shade of madness in the eye of the owner that made Vijay very uncomfortable. He drove toward home unusually fast.

The events in the capital, New Delhi, evolved rapidly. The prime minister's office could not be vacant for long, and the ruling party had to pick a successor. So, Indira's elder son, Rajiv Gandhi, was immediately brought to the capital and was sworn in as India's next prime minister by the president, Giani Zail Singh, who was a Sikh.

Rajiv Gandhi was the reluctant heir to the Nehru-Gandhi throne. Indira had hoped her younger son, Sanjay Gandhi, would be the one to succeed her. He was Indira's right-hand man during the period of emergency. On the other hand, Rajiv, an airline pilot, was happily married and leading a peaceful life out of the public eye. Sanjay unexpectedly died when doing acrobatics in his private plane went wrong, and the plane crashed. His death broke Indira from within. She called for Rajiv to come and take the place of his brother, against his wishes to join politics.

Rajiv Gandhi's swearing-in announcement was met with strong opposition in Punjab. Many thought that they were back to square one. They'd just gotten rid of Indira, and the government now put her son in charge. This was supposed to be a democracy and not a monarchy. The news had dampened the celebrations across Punjab.

Vijay and his family stayed inside the home as the noise of fireworks, bhangra, and *dhol* continued through the night. Despite Rajiv Gandhi's taking office, the real trouble had only started. As the celebrations of Indira's death progressed in Punjab, so did the aggression against the Sikhs outside Punjab.

In Punjab, devotees gathered outside the gurdwaras in hordes, celebrating avenging the attack on the Golden Temple. They illuminated gurdwaras with candles. Roadside tents popped up and were distributing sweets and tea to passersby. Volunteers stopped all cars on the roads and distributed ladoos or prasad to the occupants. Any refusal to accept their offering of food and sweets instigated an altercation, forcing vehicle occupants to comply.

The situation in Delhi and other cities outside Punjab degraded. Indira supporters were angry, and news of celebrations in Punjab only fuelled the fire. In Delhi, reports were spreading that many local leaders from the ruling party planned to attack Sikh communities in retaliation for Indira's murder.

Over the next few days, the glorious city witnessed its history's darkest and most shameful hours. Thousands of families were destroyed, and many more were displaced from their homes. This period of Delhi's history will fester in hearts for many decades to come. It will put a black mark on India's magnificent history. The virtues of tolerance and ahimsa— nonviolence, were abandoned, and the land of Gautama Buddha, the land of Mahatma Gandhi, will be forever tarnished by what happened next.

14

November 1984: Delhi Massacre

The Sikh community in Punjab knew their fellow Sikhs living in Delhi may become the target of reprisals for Indira's death. There was a palpable sense of unease, a feeling that something terrible was about to happen.

On the morning of November 1, 1984, the autumn breeze blew across Patiala, carrying a light chill, hinting at the impending winter. It was a clear day, and the sun shone bright, illuminating the city with its warm glow. But the warmth and light were not to stay for a long time.

Vijay and Renu were at home in Patiala, watching the news. The broadcast featured the preparation of Indira Gandhi's last rites. Vijay wanted to go to his office, but Renu stopped him. For once, he listened to her and stayed back. Schools were closed, and Chetan and Vikki were at home as well. The administration had declared a one-week mourning period, and all schools and government offices were closed. No curfew was imposed yet, but people were advised not to step outside their homes unless absolutely necessary. Vijay and Renu deliberated what might come next.

"This is not a good situation. Violence and killings will rise again." Vijay was shaking his head as he sat in front of the TV, the newspaper in his hand.

"I am scared to go anywhere."

Renu, visibly nervous, sauntered between the kitchen and her bedroom. It was time for her morning walk outside, but she decided to stay inside today. Going out did not seem like a good idea. Her head hung low, and she took deep sighs after every few minutes.

Frightened, Chetan watched his parents as he stood beside their bedroom door. As the day progressed, shocking news started to arrive from Delhi. It began with reports of a few killings, but soon, the news of a full-blown riot engulfing the city of Delhi reached Patiala. Vijay and Renu once again started calling all their relatives.

Vijay called his sister's home in Delhi to check on her and to learn more about the situation there. It took a dozen tries before he got through.

"Hello, Didi, how are things in Delhi?" he asked.

"Not good."

"What's happening? We are hearing about riots in Delhi. Is that true?"

"Yes, it is awful here." She was sobbing as she started to describe the situation.

What Vijay heard shook him to the core. At the instructions of local leaders, citizens carried out indiscriminate killings of Sikhs in Delhi.

The ruling party leaders in Delhi met with supporters and goons and distributed weapons and money. The party workers paid them to kill Sikhs and destroy their businesses. The mobs on foot, in cars, and on motorbikes swarmed across the city and started their killing spree. Perpetrators carried iron rods, knives, and kerosene to kill and burn. Marauding mobs entered colonies with Sikh communities, killing Sikh men and destroying their shops and houses. They stopped buses and trains in and near Delhi, pulling off passengers and burning them alive. Men, women, and children were dragged from their homes, pulled by their hair, and beaten or hacked on the streets. They put tires around the necks of men and lit them on fire. The death toll rose rapidly. News of the massacre reached every corner of India. No one had ever seen, heard, or experienced such terror since the partition of India in 1947.

Chetan was in the room with Vijay and Renu, with the TV still on. The sound of commotion in the street was getting louder, and people were out of their homes and inquiring about the well-being of others' relatives in Delhi. Usually, Renu would have stepped out and become a part of conversations. However, today, she did not dare to face the landlady. Mrs. Randhawa stood outside the house with a few other neighbors. Chetan watched her from his bedroom window. Her voice was loud, and her face was full of anger and disgust. Her chest heaved as she spoke, and her arms moved aggressively in all directions.

"Is there no justice left in this country? Has the Congress Party lost all decency and conscience? What are they thinking? Killing Sikhs will have repercussions. Have they not learned their lesson?"

She was agitated but then started to channel her anger into action. The discussion morphed from angry talk to preparing to help those suffering in Delhi. She suggested that everyone from the neighborhood visit the gurdwara and figure out how to help the displaced. She discussed plans for setting up camps inside the gurdwara and creating places to stay for anyone coming to Patiala from Delhi and other impacted cities nationwide.

Chetan went to his room and curled under his blanket, trying to distract himself with a comic book. He was not able to read and just kept staring at the pages. He again felt the fear of death so close to him. Occasionally, he closed his eyes and mumbled prayers. It was afternoon, but he desperately wanted to go to sleep, hoping all would be well once he woke up. But he was too anxious to go to sleep. He wanted to cry but could not. His eyes shifted between the books and the photo frames of several gods on his room shelf. His ears were set on the conversation between Vijay and Renu and the loud voices outside the house.

Renu could not stay inside any longer and exited the house's back door and walked toward the front gate. She was face-to-face with the landlady. Renu looked at her, partly filled with guilt and partly pleading.

"You do not have to worry. You are safe here." Mrs. Randhawa sensed Renu's fear and assured her again. Her voice was assertive, but there was anger. "Call us at any time if you feel any threat. Sardar Ji and I will come down." Her face was grave. The smiles were gone, but she meant every word that she said.

"I need to make preparations for the gurdwara." Mrs. Randhawa left for her home upstairs.

Renu did not know what to say; she just folded her hands, showing her gratitude. Renu was left alone. She walked to the backyard and started pacing on the red brick floor while Vijay stayed inside, glued to the TV.

In the days that followed, Delhi struggled to come to terms

147

with the enormity of what had happened. Over five thousand were killed across the country, and tens of thousands were displaced from their homes. Hundreds of families migrated from Delhi to Punjab to secure their survival and safety. The administration in Delhi was indifferent and in no hurry to bring the perpetrators to justice.

"When a large tree falls," they said, "the earth is bound to shake."

A few weeks had passed by, but the horror of the massacre and the enormity of loss was not subsiding. The fear, the repulsion, and the guilt lingered on.

It was about six thirty in the evening and already dark outside. Vijay was back from his office. He had just gotten off the phone and was talking to Renu. Chetan had his eyes on his schoolbooks, but half his attention was on what Vijay was saying. They were talking about meeting someone, but Renu seemed very reluctant.

"Chetan, get ready and come with me," Vijay said.

"Where are we going?"

"To meet someone."

"Where?"

"Just get ready quickly."

Chetan quickly changed his sweater, combed his curly hair, and put his slippers on. He was wearing woolen socks, and his heels were an inch and a half outside the slippers. Vijay gave his outfit a glance and looked away. He picked up the *tokari*, a green plastic basket with two white handles. In the basket were three small steel containers and one large one.

Chetan and Vijay sat inside the car, which had been sitting outside for a while. Its beige rexine seats were cold, which gave Chetan an instant shiver. The vehicle did not have any

148

heating. He curled a little and put his hands on the warm steel containers inside the *tokari*.

They stopped in front of a white-painted house with a yellow front gate. It was barely ten minutes from home, but the drive seemed much longer. There was no exchange of words between them. Chetan was very familiar with this house. It was Bhushan Uncle's home. He was slightly surprised, as the uncle and his family had moved out of this house a few days back. They had moved to Delhi.

Chetan looked at his father. "Are we meeting Bhushan Uncle?"

"No. They are gone," said Vijay as he stepped out of the car. Chetan followed.

Vijay went toward the main gate and rang the doorbell. Chetan could see some commotion inside the house. He could see through the windows where curtains had previously hung.

After a few minutes, a confused Sikh gentleman appeared at the front door. He wore a sky-blue turban, a kurta-pajama ensemble, and a brown-colored, hand-knitted woolen vest. He was taller and heavier than Vijay. His turban was slightly askew, and the exhaustion etched on his bearded face. His long beard, usually meticulously maintained, was untied and bore traces of dust and sweat, narrating the silent story of turmoil. He did not seem to like the two being there.

"Haan ji, who are you looking for?" the man asked in a sharp tone, squinting his eyes. He was still behind the gate and hesitant to open it.

"Are you Sardar Balbir Singh?" Vijay inquired.

"Yes, how can I help you?" Balbir's brow furrowed beneath his turban, and a flicker of uncertainty danced in his gaze. The weariness that had clung to him moments ago now mingled

149

with a sense of bewilderment, leaving him grappling with questions in the flickering light of the doorway.

"*Sat Sri Akaal ji*. My name is Vijay. We have brought some food," Vijay said with a sheepish and very cautious smile. "How was your journey from Delhi?"

He looked into Balbir's eyes and immediately regretted asking that question. He very well knew the horror Balbir Singh had just escaped.

Balbir replied with nothing more than a stare.

15

Balbir Singh

In the bustling neighborhood of Narayana, Delhi, lived a strikingly handsome Sikh man named Balbir Singh. Balbir Singh was the pillar of Narayana *mohalla* and had lived in the area for over thirty-five years. He was born in Pakpattan, a holy city, the land of Baba Farid, which is now in Pakistan. Balbir made Delhi home when he moved there with his parents in 1947. He was five at that time. The move to Delhi was neither pleasant nor voluntary. His family was one of the thousands of refugee families who were pushed out of the newly created Muslim-majority Pakistan.

Balbir stood tall; his lean and athletic build was a testament to his disciplined lifestyle. His dark, long hair, neatly tied in a turban, exuded an aura of reverence and tradition. A well-groomed beard framed his face, accentuating his strong jawline and adding to his magnetic appeal. His expressive, dark eyes shone with deep wisdom and kindness. Always clothed in simple traditional attire, Balbir effortlessly blended tradition with modernity. His impeccably tailored kurta-pajama ensemble, complemented by a stylish waistcoat, showcased his innate discipline and his attention to proper raiment. He proudly wore his heritage, adorning himself with a small, intricately designed kirpan—a dagger symbolizing his Sikh faith.

Beyond his physical appearance, Balbir possessed an inherent aura of grace and humility. He carried himself with poise and confidence, yet remained grounded and approachable. Balbir was full of life, brave, and had a never-say-die spirit that infused life into even the dreariest people. He was a beacon of charm and grace, captivating those around him with his dignified presence and warm smile. His commitment to helping others was evident in his involvement with local community initiatives, where he tirelessly worked toward uplifting the underprivileged and fostering harmony. Always eager to help, he stood by his neighbors through thick and thin. He could be seen aiding in neighborhood weddings, arranging cooking gas for someone, or getting a ration card renewed for an elderly lady; he was always there for his community. But life for him was anything but a bed of roses. His courage and sense of service came from the years of struggle he and his family endured.

The British Raj prevailed from 1858 to 1947, a period of colonial rule in India. During this time, the British exploited India's resources, divided the population along religious and caste lines, and suppressed dissent. As the British prepared to leave India in 1947, they faced a daunting challenge: transferring power to the Indian leaders without triggering a civil war. The Muslim League, led by Mohammed Ali Jinnah, had demanded a separate nation for Muslims, arguing that they would not be safe in a Hindu-dominated India. On the other hand, the Indian National Congress, led by Mahatma

Gandhi and Jawaharlal Nehru, initially opposed the idea of a separate nation and advocated for a united, secular India.

With no path forward for a unified nation, Lord Mountbatten, the last viceroy of India, proposed a plan to partition British India into two independent states: India and Pakistan. Eventually, the plan was accepted by the Congress Party and the Muslim League. In August 1947, India and Pakistan became independent nations. The partition of British India into Pakistan and India in 1947 was one of the most traumatic episodes in the subcontinent's history. It led to the displacement of millions of people, the death of hundreds of thousands, and the creation of two nations, which would shape the region's political and cultural landscape for decades. The partition was accompanied by massive violence and bloodshed. Millions of Hindus and Muslims were forced to flee their homes and cross the border to the newly created India or Pakistan. Communal riots broke out across the subcontinent as the migration started. The violence was particularly intense in Punjab and Bengal, where the two nations were carved out of a region with a mixed population of Hindus, Muslims, and Sikhs.

Balbir Singh was born in 1942 into a Sikh family who lived in the Muslim-majority region. Balbir's father, whom he called Papa Ji, was a wealthy Sikh landlord with hundreds of acres of agricultural land in that Muslim-majority area of British India. Everyone called him Rai Sahib, a title he got from a British official. Balbir's father moved around in high society, wearing his turban and immaculate black suit.

The partition saw the loss of everything Papa Ji had: his land, money, mansions, servants, and cooks. He delayed his move to the Indian side as long as possible. He hoped to stay in his ancestral land with some change of fate. It was inconceivable for him to leave his land, where he reigned almost as a king, and move to a strange place where he knew no one. But the violence kept coming closer to home, and he and his wife made the tough decision to migrate to the Indian side. They left all their wealth and power, took their three children, and joined the millions to move to India. Balbir was the youngest of the three children. He had a brother who was ten years older than him and a sister three years older. The move was not easy. The path to India was littered with bloodshed, dead bodies, fire, and riots. That was the first arduous journey of Balbir's life, but unfortunately, it would not be his last.

Balbir was about four years old when he arrived in Delhi, India, with his family and thousands of other refugees. They had to leave everything behind: land, servants, cattle, bunga-lows, everything. On arrival, they were allocated a tent in a refugee camp, a far cry from the palatial home they were used to. They waited their turn for a government-alloted house, a place they could call home. Balbir's father had lost everything but his dignity. He did not have time to rest or lament over what was lost. The responsibility to feed the family got him to work right away. His courage and the resolve to build his fortunes back remained intact. He was not a man who wasted time feeling sorry for himself. Still wearing his black suit daily, he knocked at government officials' doors to get allotted a house and a business place.

The government assigned them a house and some farmland near Punjab, but the family decided to stay in Delhi. They felt safe there. Balbir's mother had saved some English gold guineas, which she hid from the looters and brought to India. Balbir's father sold them and used the money to start a new business in Delhi's Lajpat Nagar market. Balbir's mother, whom he called Biji, was emotionally devastated by the move. She had lost all her help, her cooks, servants, cars, and the driver. She had lost the prestige she enjoyed back home, where people were ready to serve her at her whim. In Delhi, she was nobody. She did not like the people she met in Delhi. Her friends, primarily Muslim women, remained in Pakistan. She missed them.

Papa Ji, on the other hand, never complained. His main purpose was to get food on the table, which he focused on. He went to his newly started business and opened the shutters of his new fabric shop in Lajpat Nagar at 10:00 a.m. sharp and closed it at eight in the evening. From there, he took a rickshaw back home. He sat on the rickshaw with the same pride and dignity as he would sit in his chauffeur-driven car.

Every Sunday, he kept the shop closed. He took the whole family to Gurdwara Bangla Sahib, where they all helped with the *langar*—the meal distribution. Helping the community was ingrained in Balbir Singh from early childhood. He joined his parents in distributing *parsada* in the meal hall and later spent time in the back kitchen washing utensils. Balbir enjoyed playing in the water while washing the dishes. The whole family would spend a few hours serving in the gurdwara and return home to prepare for the next week.

Everyone in the family was coping with the change in their own way. Settling into the new place was not easy. Balbir's father kept himself busy with work, and his mother cared for the household and kids. However, she complained all the time about the fortunes they had lost. His elder sister and brother were busy with their studies, and Balbir was too young to understand the tragedy the family had just experienced. He was still his normal self, but his elder brother, Satbir, sank into a deep depression and remained aloof. Satbir stopped talking to anyone at home. He blamed Papa Ji for the family's new wretched state. He was always angry and frequently got into fights with neighbors or classmates. Then, upon being sent home from school, arguments with his mother ensued.

In the winter of 1948, a little over a year after they moved to Delhi, Satbir jumped headfirst from the roof of their house. He died instantly. The shock of Satbir's death was too much for the family. His mother and sisters cried for weeks, and his father became a ghost of his former glory. Balbir had lost his protector, the brother who took little Balbir out for bicycle rides and defended him from the neighborhood bullies. An extreme sadness came over the family and never went away.

Work went back to routine for Papa Ji—the shop, the home, and the gurdwara. He was broken but had no choice but to keep moving forward. He aged quickly and was not in good health. Ultimately, Papa Ji died of a massive heart attack in 1959, soon after Balbir's seventeenth birthday. His dream of building back his fortune remained unfulfilled.

The burden of being the bread earner and running the household came on Balbir's young shoulders. He had to take care of his emotionally fragile mother and a young sister. He left his studies and started to look after the family shop. He had some experience managing the business—whatever he had learned from his father—and the rest he would have to pick up on his own. Lenders came after him, and people who owed them money refused to pay. Making ends meet became a daily struggle for Balbir.

Over time, he rebuilt and expanded his business. His daily routine mirrored his father's disciplined nature. Rising before dawn, he would start the day with a bath and prayers. With an unwavering devotion to his faith, he engaged in selfless service, embracing the Sikh principles of *seva* and charity. He connected with suppliers from Panipat and Ludhiana and expanded his clientele. He had a knack for making the people around him comfortable. He displayed equal ease whether selling to a twenty-five-year-old woman or a sixty-five-year-old grandmother. He built relationships with his clients, helping families build a trousseau for a bride or checking back on the regulars for their clothing needs every summer and winter. His business picked up, and he saved enough money to marry his sister to a nice guy from Delhi. After a long time, during her wedding, Balbir felt happy and proud.

The very day after the sister's wedding, Biji began pestering him.

"Now, I need to find a pretty girl for you."

"Nah, Biji, not now. We do not have the money to feed another family member,"

"Girls come with their destiny. You see, once you marry, things will change for good."

"How do you know, Biji? What if she fights with you and throws you out of the house?" Balbir chuckled.

"Not possible. I'll keep her as my daughter."

"We'll talk later."

"I do not want to die without seeing my grandson's face." An ultimatum that every Indian mother gives to a son who is not ready for marriage. "I have even found a girl for you."

Balbir arched an amused eyebrow. "Really? You have been looking for girls for me without even asking me?"

"What is there to ask? I know your choice, and what's best for you."

"Okay, Biji, as you feel right. But, I am not marrying for another two years."

Biji had her mind set on a girl, Nirmal, from Amritsar. She was from a well-to-do business family who had lived in the city for many generations. They were not refugees like Balbir and his mother. It took much convincing from his mother to get the girl's parents to accept this relationship. No one would give their daughter to refugees. Even after twenty-plus years of migrating to India, they were considered outsiders.

Getting acceptance was difficult for people who migrated from Pakistan. People blamed refugees like Balbir for the increased crime rate in the city. Refugees were blamed for stealing the government-allocated land from the rightful owners. They were labeled freeloaders and Pakistan sympathizers and were seldom invited into homes. They remained people with no nation for a long time. Refugees were like strangers at home and were always looked at with suspicion. Whenever a theft occurred in the neighborhood, the police started the investigation at one of their houses. They did not have much voice and tolerated mistreatment and insults from everyone around them. The rich lives of their past did not seem to matter anymore.

In their new homes, they were at the mercy of the government and the people around them, pushed into this miserable situation through no fault of their own. And, even after years of settlement, they were still looked at with suspicion and as outsiders.

It was a routine thing for Balbir to visit the police station. Sometimes, he was whisked away to be interrogated about a crime, and sometimes, he would go voluntarily to help one of the erstwhile refugees and get them released from jail. He was comfortable in front of the authorities. His courage and collected manner enabled him to win favors with the local police officers. He was now one of the police's advisers and a community leader that the police could depend on.

Biji wanted to ensure that Balbir had a better life than other migrants from Pakistan. Marriage was a chance to bring him into the mainstream, and she tried to ensure that he got a fair chance at rebuilding his life and bringing back the family's honor. Some common relatives got involved, and the boy's pedigree was hard to ignore. Moreover, he was tall, handsome, and a fair-skinned Sikh boy who knew how to win people's hearts.

Balbir married in February 1970. Nirmal was everything Balbir imagined in a life partner. She was strong, business savvy, cheerful, and so beautiful. Everyone in the neighborhood talked about Balbir's gorgeous bride and how lucky he was to marry a girl from a well-to-do family from Amritsar.

Nirmal took no time to take over the household and often offered business advice to Balbir.

"I need to go to Panipat to get some fabrics," said Balbir.

"Why? Why not go to Karnal? You will find them at a much cheaper price and from the source. There are a few mills there."

"And this is a good time to visit Ludhiana to lock in your rates for the winter. If you go later, the prices will be much higher." Nirmal had a knack for negotiation and sourcing, and Balbir found a great partner in her. Moreover, her father and a vast network of relatives put Balbir in touch with many new customers, and his business flourished.

About one year after the wedding, in April 1971, their first daughter, Babli, was born. Life was getting smoother. Money was not a problem anymore. They moved into a bigger and newer house, and Balbir bought a new scooter to commute to his shop and business partners.

In June 1973, a second daughter, Simran, was born. She was the most beautiful child Balbir had ever seen. The first time he took her in his arms, his heart melted. He cried uncontrollably, unsure as to what had come over him. After a long time, he missed having Papa Ji around. He'd never gotten this feeling when Babli was born. Maybe he was too busy to be emotionally available a few years back and could not give himself permission to pause and marvel at the birth of his first child. However, he was now at a different stage in life, and he was thankful. Biji was not exactly happy about Simran's birth, a second girl grandchild. Like any Indian grandmother, she was looking for a grandson. But Simran was the apple of Balbir's eye. She could do no wrong.

Biji was not one to give up so easily. She kept insisting on a grandson.

"You should give it another try to have a son!"

"Biji, I do not want another child. It is costly to raise kids these days."

"Every child comes with their destiny." The same logic came back.

"I want to give a good life and education to my children. There is no difference between boys and girls these days."

"Why is there no difference? Who will carry your and your Papa Ji's name? Your brother also left us so soon, and now you will not have a son." Good old emotional blackmail.

"Biji, do not bring Papa Ji and Vir Ji into this."

"Even Bhen Ji has two grandsons. I do not want to be left out." Biji pointed toward the house across the street, occupied by an old lady who had become her close friend.

160

"So, should I have another child so you can compete with the neighbors?"

"Think who will give fire to you when you die?" The final blow.

These discussions became increasingly regular, and finally, in 1976, Raju was born. Biji was on cloud nine. She invited everyone from the neighborhood to show off her grandson as if her life's purpose was now fulfilled. Babli and Simran were so thrilled to have a baby brother. Raju was their new toy.

"Maybe having another child is not that bad, after all," Balbir said.

"No, we'll manage. I always wanted three kids." Nirmal was happy. She looked even more beautiful.

Life was running on a comfortable path. The kids were going to school. Still, Biji missed her home in Pakistan. She would tell stories to all about how big their mansion was. She would boast to her friends about her servants, the three horses, and the eight cows they had back in the day. She missed those large gatherings at her house, now in Pakistan, and the finger-licking food prepared by their *khansamah*, the head cook. She would always complain about the food in Delhi.

"They need to learn how to cook here."

"All the good cooks are in Pakistan. No hotel or restaurant knows how to make a decent mutton biryani."

"Can someone find a place that sells tosha? The karachi halwa you get in Delhi is an insult to the name." She had still not reconciled to the fact that they were driven out of their homes. She never would.

A few relatively peaceful years passed. And then came 1984. Babli was now in the eighth grade, Simran in the sixth, and the youngest, Raju, the favorite of Biji, was in the third class.

They were going to a private school just a short distance from home. The parents were committed to providing the best education and did not send them to a government school. Babli was studious and always came first in her class; to the contrary, Simran was much more involved in extracurriculars besides her studies. She was good in academics but had her hands in various activities, such as singing, debate, sports, and whatever she could do. She was always the favorite of her teachers. Balbir had a special corner for her in his heart. She would always bring a smile to his face and knew what buttons to press to get all her wishes granted.

Raju, though, was turning out to be a spoiled brat. He never dared to misbehave in front of Balbir, but in his absence, he would run the house as a prince with all due support from his grandmother. Grandmother would shower him with gifts, clothes, toys, and sweets. Raju would run to Biji crying whenever he did not get this way with Nirmal or his sisters. For the sisters, he became a menace.

Balbir was not one to get involved in politics. He was a businessman. He was a family man. He wanted to care for his business and family, but things would change again.

Another storm was brewing and would burst in November 1984.

16

November 1984: In the Middle of the Massacre

October 31, 1984 began as just another Delhi autumn day. In the bustling market of Lajpat Nagar, people went about their business, haggling with shopkeepers and bargaining over saris and shoes. The air was filled with the smell of punjabi kachori and chole bhature, and the sounds of honking cars and shouting vendors indicated business as usual. By the evening, Delhi was on the edge of devastation.

The assassination of India's prime minister, Indira Gandhi, by her bodyguards shocked the nation, igniting a wave of tension and fear. The news plunged the country into mourning, but a pot of vitriol was brewing beneath the surface. Hundreds gathered around the hospital where Indira's body was kept and began shouting slogans of vengeance. The undercurrents of violence had started to form. The shock, anger, fear, and utter helplessness could be seen across the crowd.

By the evening of October 31, the markets got quieter than usual. The shopkeepers huddled together, talking in hushed tones. The streets were almost devoid of activity, except for a handful of stray dogs and cats. In the posh neighborhoods of South Delhi, the wealthy mourned the death of Indira in their own way. They held private vigils and candlelight gatherings and expressed their condolences to the family of the slain prime minister. But even the most peaceful mind could feel the tensions brewing, a feeling that the calm would not last. At the local gurdwara, the leaders urged the community to remain strong and vigilant. But their words had a sense of trepidation, as if they anticipated that something horrid was about to happen.

Balbir, being a Sikh, sensed the impending danger and knew that he had to tread cautiously on his way back home. He hesitated to close his shop early but could sense that the situation was critical. He was not one to run away from danger, but what had happened was unprecedented, and he feared a backlash. Many shopkeepers had already left by 3:30 p.m. Balbir waited another hour to see if he'd get any customers, but the streets were almost deserted. Finally, he reluctantly brought the shop's shutter down and started toward his home.

Mounting his trusty scooter, Balbir set off on his usual route, but the atmosphere was different that evening. The once bustling streets now seemed eerily silent, except for sporadic bursts of commotion and the distant sounds of angry voices. As he maneuvered through the labyrinthine lanes, he encountered agitated crowds, their emotions running high and their expressions filled with anger and confusion. Many shouted slogans extolling Indira, while others clamored for revenge.

The sight of Balbir, with his turban and beard, attracted attention amid the charged atmosphere. Shouts and derogatory remarks were hurled toward him, piercing the air with hostility. Fear gripped his heart, but Balbir maintained his composure, relying on his inner strength and resilience, and kept driving.

But then, someone hurled a big stone at him, screaming. "Kill that bastard!"

"We'll take our revenge!" shouted another one.

The rock hit the rear end of his scooter. Balbir picked up his pace and started to rush back home. With every yard crossed, Balbir's anxiousness increased. He held the scooter handlebars ever more tightly, determined to reach home quickly. He knew that reaching home safely was paramount for his own well-being and for Nirmal and Biji's peace of mind. They must be distraught and afraid after learning everything happening in various parts of Delhi. As he navigated the narrow streets, he encountered roadblocks hastily erected by angry mobs. The tension in the air was palpable, and he had to exercise caution to avoid confrontations. He was thinking about Nirmal and their children—Babli, Simran, and Raju.

They must be back from school by now. Hope they are staying inside the home.

Balbir's face remained stoic, betraying the storm of the fear and apprehension that churned within him. His eyes focused intently on the road ahead, searching for alternative routes and safe passages to steer clear of potential trouble. He relied on his knowledge of the area, skillfully maneuvering through neighborhood back alleys and by-lanes, taking detours whenever necessary. Balbir's heart raced with each passing moment, and he fervently prayed for the safety of his family and community and hoped that the storm of anger would subside. Deep within, he carried a glimmer of optimism, believing that goodness and reason would eventually prevail over anger, resentment, and violence.

Finally, after what felt like an eternity, Balbir reached the safety of his home. His shoulders sagged with relief, but his mind remained consumed by the unfolding events. He rang the doorbell.

Nirmal lept and hugged him as soon as she opened the door. "Thank God, you are home." Biji was on the sofa with her eyes glued to the entryway, moving prayer beads in her hand and mumbling.

"The kids?" Balbir asked as he shut the door behind him.

"Safe in their rooms."

The evening sky turned darker, mirroring the unsettling atmosphere that engulfed the city. The usual cacophony of everyday life was replaced by the sound of distant sirens and occasional car horns. The streets seemed deserted, but the tension remained. As October 31 ended, a palpable terror hung in the air like a heavy fog.

The following morning, as the sun rose on the city, the simmering tensions erupted into a horrifying wave of violence. Balbir woke to the news that the riots had begun. Crowds, fueled by anger and hatred, roamed the streets, targeting Sikh men and attacking their homes and businesses.

In the neighborhoods of East Delhi, the violence was particularly intense. Gangs instigated and armed by local leaders charged any Sikh person in sight with sticks and stones. The air was thick with smoke from burning tires and buses against the background sound of shattering glass as rioters kept destroying shops and homes. The first person was killed in East Delhi. Then, they began to swarm across all corners of Delhi. Tempers boiling, they ran towards any Sikh they saw, faces twisted with rage and spouting venom as they sought vengeance for the assassination of Indira.

The police were outnumbered and had instructions to stay out of the way. Ambulances rushed through the streets, sirens blaring as they tried to reach the wounded and the dying.

Soon, the news arrived that rioters were approaching Balbir Singh's neighborhood. He and his family were the target. Amid the chaos and panic, Balbir found himself and his family fighting for survival. They were locked inside their home, in shock, as were many others, when Balbir's neighbor of fifteen years, Mr. Mittal, came running to their place. He knew that immediate action was necessary to keep Balbir and his family alive.

"Balbir Ji, come and hide in our home."

"Hide?" The thought of hiding was anathema to Balbir. He was still thinking that he could save his family on his own.

"No, we'll be okay," he said.

"This is not the time for pride, Balbir," the neighbor shouted. "Think about your family. You will not be able to fight a mob of hundreds of people."

Despite his anger, Balbir knew his neighbor was right. So, he rushed inside the home.

"Biji, kids, let's go to Mittal Ji's palace for the night."

"Why?" Biji asked. The days of the 1947 partition flashed before her eyes. Her voice was quivering with fear.

"Let's hurry." Balbir grabbed Nirmal's hand, wrapped his other arm around the girls, and rushed. Biji followed, holding Raju's hand by her side. They left the door open as an offering to the rioters.

As the violent throngs drew closer to their neighborhood, the air was thick with smoke, echoing the sounds of chaos.

The once peaceful streets transformed into a battleground of hatred and aggression. Balbir and his family huddled in Mr. Mittal's house, their hearts pounding with fear.

The night was the longest one of their lives. The atmosphere inside Mr. Mittal's house grew tense as the noise of the wild crowd, the clinking of swords and iron rods, and their shouts and abuses filled the air. They attacked the colony at around 10:30 p.m. They were looking for Balbir. The neighbors told the attackers that he had run away in the morning. After searching through the streets, they were still unconvinced. They returned to Balbir's home, ransacked every corner, and destroyed every piece of furniture and every appliance. With each minute, the attacks outside grew louder and more frenzied. The mob, driven by a destructive insanity, continued its rampage, leaving devastation in its wake. The sound of breaking glass and the crackling of fires surrounded Balbir as he tried to accept his safe haven, his home, was being destroyed next door, and he could do nothing about it. He just sat there helpless and unable to make eye contact with Nirmal or his mother.

By the time the November 2 sun rose over Delhi, the city was in ruins. People woke to streets littered with debris, the air thick with smoke and ash, and the smell of burning buildings and dead bodies lingering in the air. The death toll was staggering, with thousands of people killed and many more injured.

Authorities announced a curfew in Delhi but did not enforce it.

As the survivors emerged from their homes, they were overwhelmed by the scenes of devastation. Their shops and homes had been destroyed, and family members were killed, injured, or missing. People lost everything they owned. Police patrolled the streets, but their presence seemed very superficial. The army was deployed in Delhi, but the local leaders and law enforcement were not cooperating to bring the violence to an end. It took days to suppress the violence, but by then, untold damage had been caused. Once again, after 1947, there were hundreds of displaced Sikhs in Delhi seeking shelter in the gurdwaras.

Balbir stayed at Mr. Mittal's house for three days. Finally, he did not want to be a burden or risk to him anymore, so Balbir and his family emerged cautiously from their hiding place. They approached their home with listless steps, hearts heavy with grief and fear, wondering what destruction waited for them in their home. Balbir's mind was already planning how to build up his life again. As his home, his shop was also destroyed in the riots. Although Balbir and his family had survived the attacks, the scars were etched on their hearts for the rest of their lives.

As Balbir and his family cautiously entered their home, they witnessed a scene of utter devastation. What was once a place filled with love, warmth, and laughs had been reduced to a heartbreaking rubble of destruction. The rampage had left their cherished abode in ruins. The home was not livable. The windows were shattered, and the beds were broken. Their humble home, a symbol of their dreams and hard work, now stood as a mere shell of its former self. The once-solid walls had cracks, shattered glass covered the floor like a mosaic of despair, and the remnants of their belongings lay scattered in disarray. The familiar rooms, once brimming with life and laughter, were now eerie and silent, haunted by the echoes of violence. The kitchen utensils were scattered all across the house. The blades of the ceiling fan were bent. The bathroom sink was on the floor. The TV lay sideways in the corner of the drawing room. All almirahs were open and ransacked. Looters looked for any cash or jewelry they could get their hands on. Nirmal had her gold bangles, earrings, and necklaces in the locker of her Godrej almirah. It was open, everything gone.

Tears welled in Nirmal's eyes as she assessed the wreckage. The home that was full of cheerful memories was now a picture of despair. The pain of witnessing her years of work and her dreams reduced to debris was almost unbearable. It felt as though a part of her identity had been torn apart, and the sense of being violated so callously settled heavily upon her. Nirmal looked at the empty safe for a moment, wiped her tears, and then quickly looked away and got to work. There was no time to lament such things.

"Babli, grab the broom," Nirmal said. "Simran, get the empty drum from the back." Nirmal did not waste any time.

Balbir joined her and began pushing furniture to make room for the cleanup. Babli and Simran joined Balbir and Nirmal to clean up and rearrange. Raju was with Biji in one corner, watching their destroyed home. They were in too much shock to assist. Balbir, Nirmal, and their two daughters spent the whole day removing debris and recovering what little they could. A few neighbors joined in for the cleanup. The home had iron window grills and wooden shutters on the windows that were intact. They could make it livable. By the evening, they had a running kitchen with the help of a borrowed gas stove and a gas cylinder. Neighbors helped Balbir to remove the broken beds and set mattresses on the floor.

But none of them slept that night.

Though we boast of being the world's largest democracy and Delhi being its national capital, the sheer mention of the incidents of 1984 anti-Sikh riots in general and the role played by Delhi Police and state machinery in particular makes our heads hang in shame in the eyes of the world polity. —Delhi High Court, 2009.

17

Starting New. Again.

In the aftermath of the devastating November 1984 riots in Delhi, the wounds ran deep, and the scars of the violence remained etched in Balbir Singh's heart and mind.

With each passing day, Balbir found it challenging to endure the devastation the city witnessed. Once vibrant and bustling, the city had transformed into a place of mistrust and anguish. The effects of the riots reverberated through the fabric of society, leaving behind a fractured community and a sense of lingering unease.

For Balbir, life took a somber tone. He was not one to run from a difficult situation, but this was beyond difficult. The thriving business he had diligently built over the years now languished, crippled by the aftermath of the riots. The once-bustling streets of his neighborhood became eerily quiet, devoid of the familiar faces and boisterous activity that had defined them. The air carried a heavy weight, filled with mistrust and the lingering remnants of the violence that had torn through the city.

Every day became a painful reminder of the communal divide exposed during those dark days. Balbir could no longer bear the glares, threats, taunts from hooligans, and not-so-subtle prejudices that had become woven into the very fabric of society. The once-welcoming streets now felt suffocating, with every step reminding him of the shattered sense of belonging he once held. Although the mass violence had subsided, the threat was still there. The neighbors who were there for each other for decades were suspicious of each other. The city was burned down, literally. Several days had passed after the curfew, but one could still smell the burned tires, find kerosene cans on the street corners, see charred shops, and witness drying blood on street corners.

The government eventually acted and provided shelter to thousands of impacted families. Many broken families, uprooted from their homes, were sent to Tilak Vihar, which came to be known as Vidhva Vihar, the Widow Colony. Every woman there had lost some male member of their family: their husband, their sons, their fathers. Amid the gloom, they tried to make sense of what just happened to them, looking for justice.

Balbir was lucky to be alive, if there still was any such thing as being lucky. He still had all his family with him. Balbir contemplated the difficult decision of leaving Delhi, seeking shelter in a place where his identity as a Sikh would not be met with judgment or hostility. Many others were doing the same. Sustaining a family of six without any income began to prove very difficult. In a few more days, it would become hard to survive. However, the thought of uprooting his family, leaving behind familiar surroundings, and forgoing a life built with hard work and dedication weighed heavily on his heart.

Of course, no crisis should go to waste. Real estate agents smelled blood. For them, this was an opportunity to make money. So, their ingenious minds devised a new scheme—the home exchange program. They would facilitate the exchange of residential property between families living in Delhi and families in Punjab who wanted to move out of Punjab. The local agent called Balbir, proposing he could get him a house in Punjab. A great place was available in Patiala, a relatively peaceful city. Balbir was told it would be an even exchange, but the agent could try getting him some additional money to help with the move. Balbir knew his house was worth much more than the house offered in Patiala, but his options were limited. He was almost at the end of the runway.

The decision to leave behind their life in Delhi and move to Punjab weighed heavily on Balbir Singh's heart as he shared his decision with the family.

"Biji, we are moving to Patiala," Balbir told his mother loud enough for the entire family to hear. The kids were perplexed, looking at each other. Nirmal was quiet, her head hanging.

"Why Patiala?" she asked hesitantly. "We could go to Amritsar, to my parents' place," she suggested, knowing very well that Balbir's decision was not open for discussion.

"Patiala is safer than Amritsar and closer to Delhi. It will be easier for us to manage the business. We'll leave in six days. The moving truck will be here. Start packing."

Nirmal did not think arguing with Balbir on the topic was wise. She understood the gravity of their predicament and recognized the need for their family's safety and the dwindling prospects for their future in Delhi.

Biji was devastated. She could not believe they had to run from their home again. Her eyes could not hold the tears. She never imagined that there would be another partition in her lifetime. The wounds of 1947 were still fresh after all these years. She had lost her land, her mansion, and her elder son once already. And now, fate was asking her to do it all over again. Having spent years of her life in Delhi and rebuilding her life here, even after losing her elder son and her husband, the thought of uprooting their lives again did not seem fair. She did not say anything. She understood the severity of the situation and the risks lingering in the riot's aftermath. She had witnessed it all too closely while migrating from Pakistan and now again in Delhi. Her sobbing was getting louder. Nirmal put her arm around Biji and took her to her room.

"Biji, whatever fate has in store for us . . ." Nirmal's words would not bring much comfort to Biji. Nothing could console her at this moment.

Simran, Babli, and Raju were confused and understandably unhappy with the prospect of leaving their friends, schools, and familiar surroundings.

"I am not going," Raju screamed.

"Quiet, Raju," Babli intervened. She knew that, if not stopped, Raju would end up on the receiving side of Nirmal's or Balbir's anger and frustration.

"But what about school? All my friends are here." The move meant leaving all his friends, forever. Raju was grappling with the thought of starting anew in an unfamiliar place.

"You can make new friends."

"But I do not want to."

"We have to go. At least for now." Babli was trying her best to placate Raju.

Balbir was listening to the conversation between the two. He was thankful Babli had this talk with Raju, as he had no patience or energy to indulge Raju's tantrums. He tried to focus on the TV, which was still miraculously working. The news lady was talking about Ronald Regan's reelection. He had just defeated the Democrat Walter Mondale. He won forty-nine of the fifty states and 525 electoral votes, a record in American history. Simran was standing in the corner of the room, looking down at the floor. She stepped closer to Balbir, looked at him for an instant, walked toward him, and quietly sat in his lap. Her head rested against his chest. She had that instinct to feel Balbir's pain and knew how to calm him down. Balbir held her tight, and tears started rolling from his eyes.

The day of the move was here. Despite the pain, their realities in Delhi were impossible to ignore. The risk of staying in a city that no longer felt safe overshadowed any hesitations they may have had about the move. Balbir's business, once a source of his pride and stability, had suffered a severe blow, and the prospects for recovery were bleak. The economic downturn, coupled with the lingering hostility toward the Sikhs, left them with little choice but to seek refuge in Punjab. Thirty-five years of memories were to be left behind. The walls that had witnessed all their struggles, given them shelter, and protected them from the elements were useless today. They were silent witnesses to the injustice. Today, they could not protect them. The walls were ashamed and begging for forgiveness. They were supposed to be strong.

The moving truck sat outside the house, and slowly, possessions began filling it up. Balbir hired a couple of people to get the truck loaded. Any remaining sofas, almirahs, trunks, utensils, and plants from their balcony that survived the mob attack were loaded onto the truck. Many neighbors came to see them and say their goodbyes. Some helped them to pack their belongings, tears in their eyes. And a few were there with smirks, happy to see them leave. The last thing Balbir loaded onto the truck was his scooter.

The family sat in a rented taxi that charged four times the normal amount to drive them to Patiala. It was risky. Balbir sat in the front passenger seat, and they went off. He did not look back. His mind was already full of details he needed to get in place when they reached Patiala. He had to restart his business, connect with his suppliers, find new customers, and find schools for the kids.

Simran and Babli slept in the car. Raju insisted on the window seat and had his head out. The wind blew through this newly cut hair. His long hair, a symbol of Sikhism, was cut to protect his life. Biji stared off into oblivion. Nirmal watched Balbir. Balbir gazed at the road ahead.

The Delhi to Patiala drive took about seven hours. Midway, the taxi driver stopped for a break at Gulshan Dhaba, a road-side restaurant in Murthal. Everyone stepped out, stretching their legs. The weather was getting cold. They all sat at the wooden table in front of the roadside restaurant and ordered chai and aloo parathas. The kids dug into the food, and it was gone in minutes. Nirmal and Balbir took a few bites. Biji did not touch the food. She had not eaten since the previous day's lunch.

"Biji, please have something. Traveling on an empty stomach is not good," Nirmal pleaded.

"No, I will vomit if I eat," Biji pushed back.

They were out of that restaurant in thirty-five minutes. People's fear of travel kept evening traffic on the highway light. Mostly trucks and military vehicles occupied the roads. In another three hours, they were in front of their new house.

The house was in Punjabi Bagh, Patiala, one of the better neighborhoods in the city. They all were standing outside the house, looking at their new place. It was much bigger than their home in Delhi. Recently whitewashed, it looked bright. And the smell of fresh quicklime still emanated from the walls.

They opened the main gate and entered the house. The truck soon followed, and they started unloading everything inside the house. Balbir had not even seen the place. They had no idea where any of the stuff would go. So, everything was unloaded in the large living room. The truck left. Everyone was sitting on whatever they could find, on the sofa, dining chair, trunk, or just a pile of clothes. Balbir and Nirmal were tired. Seven hours of travel and then unloading and moving items indoors took its toll. Balbir was breathing heavily, standing up and gazing around the house to make sense of everything. Nirmal was thinking about dinner. It was getting dark, about eight in the evening. The kids were getting hungry, but the kitchen still required setup. She wiped her forehead with her *dupatta*, which was dusty by now, and tried to look for some plates.

"Let me arrange some food," said Balbir, his breath still heavy.

He did not know his way around the city and needed to figure out where to look for food.

"Where are you going to get food?" Nirmal did not want him to leave the house at this time.

"I'll ask around. I saw a couple of *dhabas* on the way."

"Biji, what would you like to eat? Dal? Rice?"

"All I want is a mattress. I'll go to sleep now."

"Don't you want to have any food?" Nirmal asked, knowing what her response would be. She did not wait for her answer and continued to pull the steel plates and spoons from a box. And then, suddenly, the doorbell rang.

Balbir frowned. "Who could that be at this hour?"

Despite his reservations, he opened the living room door and went out. Two people waited at the main gate, a man accompanied by a young boy.

Balbir did not particularly want to greet visitors. Today, he felt less of a husband, less of a son, and less of a father. He was ashamed that he had to run away. He wanted to hide in this new place, but somehow, someone found him out so soon.

"*Sat Sri Akaal ji.* My name is Vijay, and this is my son, Chetan. We have brought some food," he said, offering a faint smile.

Balbir furrowed his brow. "Do you know us?"

"No, but Bhushan Ji called to tell us that you would be arriving today and to see if all is safe with you," Vijay said as Chetan stood by his side and looked at Balbir.

Vijay was looking into Balbir's eyes, which were bloodshot and red. He was unsure if it was because of the long travel, sleeplessness of the last few days, or anger. It could be a bit of everything.

Bhushan was married to Vijay's niece, daughter of his eldest sister, but he was about Vijay's age. They were good friends. Bhushan had always wanted to move to Delhi. When an agent contacted him with an opportunity to exchange his Patiala home for a house in Delhi, he could not refuse. A chance to afford a house in Narayana, Delhi, could not be ignored. He agreed to swap his house with Balbir's—a great deal from any angle. Balbir's home would be valued more than twice Bhushan's in good times. But these were not good times.

Even so, Balbir invited him inside.

"*Sat Sri Akaal,*" Vijay greeted everyone in the living room, who were now staring at him in awkward silence.

Vijay knew they'd come from the worst of situations and had

just had the most miserable journey of their lives. Nirmal just bowed her head very slightly, responding to Vijay's greeting. Biji ignored him. The kids were confused and kept quiet, except Simran.

"*Sat Sri Akaal*, Uncle Ji," she returned his greetings.

"God bless you, *beta*." Vijay was happy that someone broke the awkward silence.

Vijay handed the food over to Nirmal. "Just something little to get you by for today."

"There was no need for this," Nirmal responded.

"It is nothing much, some dal, sabzi, and roti," Vijay said without looking into her eyes.

He turned to Balbir. "Here is my phone number in case you need anything later," he said, handing him a business card.

Vijay and Chetan stood there, filled with guilt, as if they were responsible for Balbir and his family's uprooting from Delhi. Nerves unsettled Chetan as he realized who the family was. He thought it was a horrible idea to go to the home of a person who was just forced out of Delhi and who may see them as the enemy.

They must hate us, he thought. *What stops them from attacking us right now?* Chetan's legs trembled. His anxiety was on the rise, and he wanted to leave the house immediately. He thought about running back into the car and waiting there. However, he looked at Simran; her slight pale smile made him stay.

"Okay, we'll leave now. Do not hesitate to call," Vijay said, folding his hands again and asking their permission to leave.

Balbir just folded his hands in response.

On his way home, Chetan wondered if Balbir's family even ate the food they brought or threw it into the garbage.

18

Simran

It was Monday, and Chetan was at school. The classroom hummed with soft noises as kids shuffled their books to get to the correct chapter. Sunlight filtered through the large windows, casting a warm glow on the cement floors. The classroom walls were adorned with vibrant posters and paintings created by the students. In the front of the class hung a picture of Jesus, right above the well-used blackboard that dominated the front of the classroom, where Ms. Sharma was carefully writing sentences with chalk, using a duster to erase and make room for new notes.

It was the third period, English class. At the front of the room stood Ms. Sharma, a senior English teacher with a passion for grammar and discipline. She wore a modest cotton sari, her hair neatly tied back in a bun, and a pair of spectacles perched on her nose. Her authoritative presence commanded respect, and her dedication to teaching was evident in every word she spoke. Ms. Sharma was going through the grammar, teaching the difference between gerunds and infinitives, when suddenly the principal was at the door. Ms. Sharma stopped in her tracks, looked at the door, and smiled.

"Hello, Sister Thomas," she addressed the principal.

"Sorry to disturb your class, Ms. Sharma. Here is a new student. The family just arrived from Delhi." Sister Thomas looked at Ms. Sharma with a glance, as if dropping a hint.

No more words were spoken, but it was understood under what circumstances this new kid was here. Many families were relocating from Delhi after the riots.

"Of course, Sister Thomas. No problems at all. We are going to take good care of her."

"What is your name, dear?"

"Simran Bajaj," the girl responded, looking up into her eyes.

Simran, a name that means "a continuous remembrance of God."

"Welcome, Simran. I am Ms. Sharma, your class teacher. Take that vacant seat over there." She pointed to the empty chair next to Chetan.

The students' seating arrangement in Ms. Sharma's classroom was carefully planned to maintain a decorum and focused atmosphere. Each desk was designed to accommodate two students, and Ms. Sharma strategically paired a boy and a girl at each desk. This arrangement was intended to keep class chatter to a minimum. She did not want two boys or two girls on the same desk to avoid talking among the students. Boys and girls did not mingle too much in the school, or that's what her assumption was.

Chetan felt a tingling inside him when Ms. Sharma pointed toward him. He had been alone at his desk for a few weeks as his fellow "benchmate" had left the school. Her father was in the army and was posted to some other station. Chetan's eyes were fixated on Simran. He remembered her from the other night. He watched her every single move as she walked toward him, almost in slow motion. She stopped beside the desk, put her school bag on it, and sat beside him. Chetan scooted a little and smiled at her.

"I'm Chetan," he whispered.

Simran kept looking straight ahead at the teacher.

"Quiet, please." Ms. Sharma ordered loudly and continued with her chapter, discussing changing gerunds to infinitives.

The recess bell rang, sweeping a wave of excitement through the classroom. Ms. Sharma gathered her belongings, reminded students to return promptly after the break, and left the room. As soon as she left, the students erupted into a joyful commotion, their energy bursting at the seams. They eagerly gathered their lunch boxes, and without a moment's hesitation, they all stormed out of the classroom, their laughter and chatter filling the corridors. Chetan was not in much of a hurry today.

"Hi, I am Chetan," he said again after gathering some courage to attempt a conversation with Simran.

"Yes, I heard the first time you said," Simran quipped.

"Do you remember me? From the other day?"

"Yes, I do." Simran looked at him and slowly started walking out of the class. Chetan stood there, watching her leave for the playground.

She is so beautiful, he thought. Simran's brown straight hair dropped to her hips, woven into a single braid, with a blue ribbon tied in a bow at the end. She had glowing fair skin and grayish-green eyes. Almost similar to Chetan's mother's eyes. Simran was of average height and thinner than other girls of her age. She walked with a straight posture that Chetan had never mastered. He always walked with somewhat of a slouch, yet another thing his mother did not like about him. Chetan studied Simran's school backpack, which she had left behind under the desk. It was bright blue with shiny metal clasps, a design you could not find in Patiala. He left the room for the basketball court, where kids played dodgeball.

The recess was over, and all the kids were back in their chairs. Chetan did not speak to Simran again for the rest of the day. As weeks passed by, Chetan and Simran were getting friendlier. She started to laugh at his silly jokes, praise his paintings, and admire his grasp on math. Math was not one of Simran's strengths. Moreover, she wanted to become a doctor, and studying math after the tenth grade was not required for pre-medical studies.

Chetan would come to school early and wait for her to arrive. Simran's father, Balbir Singh, was not very comfortable sending the kids to school alone. He accompanied them daily to school, made sure they entered the gates, and then went to his work. Babli and Simran were getting used to wearing *salwar kameez* rather than shirts and skirts, typical uniforms for girls in Delhi schools. In Punjab, the skirts in school uniforms were replaced with traditional *salwar kameez*, considered a more modest Punjabi attire. It was a result of an agreement between insurgents, local administrations, and student unions that schools were forced to comply with. White half-sleeved shirts were replaced with collared full-sleeved white *kameez*, a tunic top that flowed down to the knees, and blue skirts were replaced by sky-blue *salwars* that were puffy and wide around the waist and narrowed to a cuffed bottom, pleated all the way in Patiala style. And neckties for girls were replaced with matching light blue *dupattas*. Even Catholic schools were forced to change their uniforms. Boys continued to wear white half-sleeved shirts with sky-blue ties and sky-blue pants.

Simran looked very pretty in her *salwar* suit, Chetan thought. Simran soon became one of the most popular kids in the class and the school. Coming from Delhi, she had that little attitude and an extrovert nature that small-town Patiala kids usually did not possess. Simran participated in debates and speech competitions, read the news during the morning assembly, and teachers often asked her to assist with collecting homework. She was equally at ease speaking with girls and boys. Chetan did not like her talking to the other boys. She was his benchmate, after all, and he was the first one she met when she arrived in Patiala. However, he would be on his most congenial behavior when she was around.

* * *

It was December, the midterms were done, and the teachers planned to distribute the answer sheets with results that week. Chetan thought he did well, but he was not sure. He was always scared that he may have overlooked some details and made some careless mistakes. The last thing he wanted was to lose marks due to some "silly mistake" like skipping a question and never getting back to it, forgetting to write his name on the answer sheet, or neglecting to convert positive to negative numbers while solving algebra equations. Those were the worst mistakes and were treated most harshly at home by Chetan's mother. He was praying that there'd be no silly mistakes this time.

The biology teacher entered the room with a stack of answer sheets in her hand. Everyone knew what that meant. Simran was anxious as well. This was her first test in this school, and she wanted to do well. She was competitive. As the teacher started distributing the papers, she was excited, tapping her feet and clenching her fist. Suddenly, out of excitement, she grasped Chetan's hand, which was resting on the side of his chair, away from everyone's sight. This was the first time a girl held his hand in the school. A warm, tingling sensation traveled across his body.

Chetan did not move his hand. He almost stopped breathing to avoid any movement that might make Simran take her hand off his. He did not want that. She held his hand for a good five minutes until the teacher called her name. She rushed to grab her answer sheet, looked at it, and had a smile on her face. She returned to the desk and proudly laid the answer sheet in front of her. She had forty-one out of fifty. Chetan had forty-five. She smiled at him, and he smiled back. He was still warm from her touch. He was in love.

After the answer sheets were distributed, the teacher started with her lesson. The topic of discussion in the biology class was pollution, and the teacher started the conversation with a catastrophic industrial accident. Before the year ended, an unfortunate event would take another big bite of flesh from the already crippled nation.

The teacher was discussing the Bhopal gas tragedy, which had happened a little over a week back, on December 3. A Union Carbide pesticide plant in Bhopal, Madhya Pradesh, had a gas leak—methyl isocyanate, a poisonous gas. The toxic gas leak spread across the sleeping city late at night, exposing over half a million people living in surrounding small towns and villages. Between three and eight thousand people died within the first two weeks of the exposure, and hundreds of thousands sustained injuries. It was the world's worst industrial disaster ever. The grim discussion about the accident and the aftermath changed the mood from excitement about getting the answer sheets to somber commiseration. The images appearing on TV and in newspapers were gruesome and especially disturbing for Chetan.

The uncertainty and unpredictability of life were very unsettling for Chetan. He kept feeling that death was always so close and could surprise him from any corner. Thoughts that he could be shot at while going to school or wither away in poisonous gas while sleeping kept him up long into the night. In his own odd way, Chetan tried to face those fears and confront the repugnant images of the Bhopal disaster. He no longer wanted to hide from them. He started cutting images from the newspaper and *India Today* magazine and built a scrapbook about the tragedy. He got angry, and he felt scared while making it, but it was his way of facing adversity and controlling his anxiety.

For Chetan, painting always took him to his happy place— away from all fear and sorrow when he was working with his brush and colors. During art class the next day, the students were painting landscapes. Chetan loved painting landscapes. His favorite one had mountains in the back and a river flowing down from the right corner of the mountains. On the right side of the river was a little hut, and big trees were on the left shore of the river.

Simran watched him as he delicately colored the mountains. He squeezed tiny dollops of color from his tube watercolors onto the plastic palette, diluted them with some clear water, dipped the brush in, and colored the mountains, the river, the hut, and the trees. Chetan was particularly proud of his tube colors, which Vijay had gotten on one of his trips abroad.

"Your mountains look so amazing," Simran said with her eyes locked on his painting.

"Thanks!"

"Can you teach me how to paint such mountains?"

Chetan looked at her. He felt a sense of pride that she asked him. "Of course! Start with outlining and fill with a very light brown color. Keep it wet. The key is not to let it dry until all colors blend in." He was in his element explaining his craft.

Not many cared about Chetan's painting skills, especially his parents. Vijay or Renu occasionally praised his creations but never encouraged him to advance his skills. They would buy him coloring supplies but kept reminding him that his focus should be on his studies. For them, art was a useless skill that would not help Chetan earn a good living. "Following your dreams" was not something a kid from an 80s middle-class Indian family could afford to do.

The paintings were done, and Simran thanked him for helping her. Her hand was on the side of her seat. Chetan's hand was beside him as well. Chetan moved a little to the right and touched Simran's hand. She did not withdraw. Their hands stayed there, touching each other for a moment, and then Simran put her hand over his. They never looked at each other. The hands stayed together for the rest of the period, motionless. Chetan's hand was getting sweaty, but he would not move it. This became their routine, holding hands in class, away from everyone's sight.

Chetan and Simran never openly expressed their love for

each other. They never sat and talked beyond schoolwork or said, "I love you." They were happy sitting beside each other, discussing homework, exams, painting, and holding hands. Chetan never asked her about her home or her life back in Delhi.

The final exams were here, and the school year ended just like that. With that, so too did their sitting together and holding hands. Chetan's heart ached for her touch, but now there was no opportunity to sit together. Simran and Chetan moved to the seventh class, where seating was not assigned. Instead, kids picked their own seats; boys sat with other boys and girls with girls. Under no circumstances would a boy sit with a girl. Suddenly, the idea of a boy and a girl sitting together was frowned upon.

Chetan had Simran's home phone number and would call her once in a while on the pretext of checking about some homework assignments. She told him it took a lot of effort, some bribes, and contacting people in the right places before her Dad could get a phone connection. Chetan's calls were short and limited to schoolwork. However, both understood the hidden reason behind the call. Being with Simran made him feel confident. She gave him the acceptance and encouragement he longed for throughout childhood. Being with her made him believe that he could be loved.

Chetan was changing. He was now twelve, getting taller and bigger, and had his mood swings. Renu's beatings were less frequent but had not completely stopped. Her subtle taunts and derision continued. All of a sudden, Renu's remarks started to invoke anger in Chetan. The fear of Renu's wrath was morphing into a desire to rebel.

One routine evening, Chetan and Vikki got into a fight. They

189

had bought a new comic book, and the fight was about who got to read it first. The verbal altercation turned into a fistfight and ended with Vikki crying. Renu came storming into their room.

"What is this ruckus about? Why are you making your brother cry?" she asked with nostrils flaring and eyes raging with anger.

"I did not do anything," Chetan said, his voice trembling, knowing what was to come next.

"Tell me the truth." Renu walked closer to him, staring into his eyes.

Chetan was almost the same height as Renu. He tried hard not to look away or to bow his head down. He kept eye contact with her, but the fear of this audacity was evident from his face.

"I am telling the truth. I did not start it," Chetan said, sobbing, but his voice was firm.

Renu lifted her hand, and it swung toward Chetan's face. But something strange happened. He caught Renu's hand just before it could land on his cheek. He was holding it tight. Chetan was shocked by what he had just done. He was looking at Renu and saw the same surprise in her eyes.

"So, are you going to fight me?"

Chetan was trembling, but there was no going back from there. Still holding Renu's wrist up in the air, from somewhere he found the courage to say, "Yes."

Renu's and Chetan's eyes locked. Tears spilled from Chetan's eyes. Renu relaxed her hand and calmly lowered it. Her frown suddenly turned into a smile. A strange smile that Chetan had never seen on her face. She did not say another word; she just turned around and went to the kitchen. That was the last time she would raise her hand to him or ridicule him. She left Chetan wondering what that smile meant. Was she, in some strange way, proud of him? Maybe she was happy Chetan finally showed some spine and stood up for himself, unlike Vijay. Chetan was growing up, or maybe Simran gave him the courage to fight back.

Another year whisked by, the eighth standard was done, and the ninth was a critical year—a foundational year to set yourself up for a successful tenth grade. The Central Board conducted the tenth-grade final examinations, and how much a student scored determined what subjects they got in eleventh. Chetan knew he must score high marks to get into the pre-engineering stream. The ninth grade was the time to start getting serious, and studies had Chetan's undivided focus. He got busy with his schoolwork and daily trips to the tutor's home for additional help with math and science. Renu was closely watching his studies and still helping Chetan prepare for the exams. The constant reminder of the criticality of the exams was overwhelming, but Chetan kept moving forward with his preparations.

The ninth grade flew by, and the date of the final exams arrived. Chetan was feeling good about the exams. He had gotten into the habit of checking and rechecking his work before he submitted his answer sheets. He always kept ten minutes toward the end to cross-check everything. He was determined to make no silly mistakes anymore. He did not realize that his OCD habit was growing stronger with the day. He had invented new rituals during his exams. A clipboard with a picture of Ganesha, four fountain pens filled with ink, and an ink bottle accompanied him to the exams. He knew that under no circumstances would he even finish one pen's ink, but his logic would succumb to his paranoia.

The last ninth-grade exam was done, and Chetan was walking with his bicycle toward the school gate. He and a couple of friends beside him discussed the answers. And then he heard someone calling his name.

"Chetan! Chetan!"

He looked back and saw Simran walking toward him. There was a sense of urgency in her pace. He asked his friends to keep walking and said he would catch up with them soon.

"Hi, Simran. How are you? How was the exam?"

"It went well. Look, I have something to tell you. I did not want to disturb your preparations, so I waited for the final paper."

"Yes, what is it?"

"We are moving back to Delhi," Simran blurted, essentially ripping off the Band-Aid.

Chetan was frozen. They had not been talking as often over the last few months, but the idea that he would not be able to see her again never occurred to him.

"Why?"

"Things are improving in Delhi, and my dad said the business is better there. Moreover, he wants me to do the tenth grade from Delhi," she said hurriedly, as if she did not want to give him a chance to ask more questions. "We were just waiting for the school year to finish."

"Well, when are you leaving?"

"In two weeks."

"Can I meet you before you leave?"

Simran was hesitant. They had never met outside the school,

and the concept of dating was uncommon, especially in a small city like Patiala.

"I'll try."

"Meet me tomorrow at three thirty at Handyman's restaurant." Chetan picked a place and time when no one would be in the restaurant, and their fathers would be out for work.

The next day, they found themselves nervously sitting inside Handyman's, a cozy restaurant known for burgers and Indo-Chinese preparations. It was their first meeting outside the school. Chetan, with his neatly combed hair and a slight smile, sat adjusting his shirt collar for what felt like the hundredth time that evening. He had picked one of his favorite blue shirts. Simran sat in front of Chetan, her eyes moving between him and the restaurant door, twirled a loose strand of hair with her fingers as she looked at him to start the conversation.

The restaurant was decorated with Hindi movie posters, old dusty lamps cast a gentle glow on walls, and slow romantic Hindi movie songs played softly in the background.

With a newfound confidence, Chetan ordered a couple of Limcas and chicken chow mein.

"Did you tell your mother?" Chetan asked.

Simran shook her head. "She thinks I am with Prableen." Another girl from their class.

"So, have you found a new school?"

"Yes, Papa got the admission confirmation a few weeks back."

As time passed, Chetan's gaze became more intense, his eyes fixed on Simran's, as if trying to convey the emotions he found hard to put into words. Simran's heart raced in response, her cheeks flushed with a mixture of excitement and nervousness.

They sat there, talking about past days, the laughs they had, the punishments Chetan got, and what was next for them.

Chetan wanted to be an engineer, and Simran a doctor. The date ended with them holding hands, fingers intertwined, one last time. As it was about to get dark, they stepped out of Handyman's, standing face-to-face to take a last look at the love they never spoke of.

"Good luck with your new school in Delhi. Call me sometimes. I'll find a way and come and meet you," Chetan said with a quivering voice.

"I'll see you, then," Simran touched his arm and waved to a waiting rickshaw puller to take her home. They parted ways, leaving a trail of laughter, stolen glances, and with the hope of keeping the promise to meet again.

19

Life as It Comes

Simran and her family moved back to Delhi in 1987, and a few months later, they sold their Patiala home. She called Chetan as soon as they reached Delhi and got a phone connection. They spoke a few more times, and then life took over. They both got busy with school and studies. Chetan continued in Patiala for his senior secondary education and started preparing for admission to an engineering college. The violence in the state appeared to be subsiding, and the news about killings was minimal. Cinemas were back in business, and travel was almost back to normal. There were no significant incidents reported across the state . . . and then there was November 10, 1989. Chetan was in the twelfth grade and deep into preparing and applying for his college admissions.

Thapar Institute of Engineering and Technology in Patiala was one of India's most reputed engineering colleges. It was a small college that generally remained quiet. Students were mostly busy with their assignments, tutorials, exams, and viva voces – the dreaded oral tests. Most students were from Punjab, but about twenty percent of the student body came from other parts of the country. Once a year, the college became highly vibrant when it hosted its annual festival, Saturnalia—an intercollege cultural festival and competition, to which various institutes from across India were invited. It was the week every student looked forward to. The preparations would start months in advance. The student body burned the midnight oil to secure sponsorships, plan events, build stages, and design meal plans. Sleeping arrangements for visitors were made in existing dorms and inside the large badminton court. That year, as every other, hundreds of students from various engineering colleges came to compete in dozens of events, ranging from music to drama to some pseudo sports– sports such as slow-cycling, where the last person to finish was the winner. Each event was scored, and at the end, all points were tabulated to declare the top three winning colleges.

However, that year, 1989, there were no winners.

The event, which was meant to be a celebration of student culture and camaraderie, was marred by the sudden eruption of violence. During the dark of the night, as students were sleeping, a few gunmen armed with AK-47s knocked down the doors of one of the dormitories. They fired on sleeping students and ended up killing nineteen visiting students. The incident sent shockwaves through the whole city and the nation. Thapar was the top engineering college on Chetan's list.

Chetan dreamed of studying there. It was not as prestigious as various Indian Institute Technology universities. However, it was still considered one of the top engineering schools in the country. Moreover, it was close to home. Whenever Chetan had some time, he and his friends visited the campus, enjoyed its lush green lawns, and played tennis on its red clay courts. He felt he belonged there. As the authorities launched an investigation to identify the perpetrators and understand the motives behind this senseless act of violence, the institute was closed, and students were sent home for an indeterminate time. Chetan sank deeper into darkness as the ghosts of evil came knocking once again.

Everything seemed unsafe once again.

After a few weeks of shock and disbelief, Chetan gathered himself and got back to preparing for the engineering entrance exams. Vijay reminded him that he could not mess up the entrance exams. One common exam that determined admission into all Punjab engineering colleges, and your results decided the course of your life. At least, it felt that way at that time. Each day was precious, and he had already lost many due to the incident. Eventually, his classes started, and he got busy with his physics, chemistry, and math classes, as well as his tuition and exam preparations.

While studying for exams, he faced another battle: his mother's ongoing sickness. Chetan's Mom had been sick for a few months now. It started with fatigue and body aches and soon developed into severe arthritis. Her disease worsened every day. Vijay took her to many doctors and traditional healers, but there was no diagnosis or relief. As Vijay was busy in his office, it became Chetan's duty to take Renu to the doctor's visits on his scooter. Many nights, she would cry in pain, and Vijay would ask Chetan to fetch a doctor in the middle of the night. Those rides along the ghostly road at night were troubling for Chetan; he had to summon all his courage to drive and knock on doctors' doors in the middle of the night.

Soon, Renu was completely bedbound. Her agonizing pain and cries late into the night tormented him and made him miserable.

Chetan would sit in her room to prepare for exams. He helped her get up and go to the bathroom, brought her meals, and made sure she took her medicine on time. The pressure of admissions and the declining health of his mother became overwhelming for Chetan. It took doctors months before they could properly diagnose her and start her on the proper medication. She had lupus. Renu's condition was deteriorating. The autoimmune disease was affecting multiple organs of her body. Her extreme fatigue, joint pains and swelling, and facial rashes were worsening.

As Chetan's exams got closer, Vijay took a month off from work to take care of Renu. This was the first time in his life he took such a long time off.

In 1990, months of grueling preparations and training culminated with finishing the engineering entrance exams. Finally, the results came, and Chetan was placed 375 out of thousands of students who took the exam. That would be good enough to get him into mechanical engineering at Thapar Institute. He was ecstatic. It was a massive win for him, a redemption after all those years of abuse at home and being ridiculed. He was proud that he finally proved his worth to Renu and Vijay. They both were on cloud nine, busy accepting congratulations from all their friends and relatives.

"If I were well, I would be dancing," Renu said. She was now completely bedridden. Her medication no longer helped. Her body was eating itself, and her organs were giving up.

She died two days after Chetan got the exam results. It seemed she was just waiting to see Chetan make it to the engineering college. Chetan and Vikki were devastated. Vijay was inconsolable. Chetan had never seen his father cry before, but Renu's death had shaken Vijay. It struck Chetan as strange. He did not find Renu and Vijay remarkably close.

What caused Vijay such pain? Was it the sense of loss? Was it the guilt?

The shock of Renu's death took everyone down. Suddenly, Chetan's joy at admission to his dream engineering college vanished. He wanted to enjoy this moment with Renu and desired some of her praises. The young boy who spent a couple of grueling years waiting for this accomplishment wanted to hear a few more times that, yes, he had done it. However, now everything seemed meaningless. His love for Renu never diminished, despite all the beatings and taunting he'd received over the years.

Chetan still needed his mother. Only she could validate his success for him. Losing her exacerbated his anxiety. His belief that he could not hold on to any happiness grew stronger. The thought that any joy was just a more enormous tragedy lurking in the corner was cemented in Chetan's psyche. From then onward, every day became a painful series of thoughts about expecting something worse to happen. Any task he started or planned was marred by the negative sentiments of death, accidents, and being caught doing something wrong.

Chetan's compulsive rituals grew more potent, and panic attacks kept occurring, but he kept pushing through his negative thoughts. All his thoughts pulled him back into darkness, but his dreams of success and his persistence to fight propelled him forward. He was more determined than ever to go far away from this place. The place that reminded him of death, destruction, and loss every day. He dreamed of leaving India after graduating and going to Germany or the United States. He hoped to start fresh and leave all the pain behind.

The engineering days were passing by quickly, but thoughts of Simran lingered. And the ache of separation only grew with time. Some evenings, memories of Simran would get more overpowering than usual, leaving Chetan's heart heavy with longing. It had been years since he'd last spoken to Simran, the undeclared love who left him behind. One such evening, he picked up the phone. He really wanted to talk to her and check how she was doing. His fingers trembled as he dialed her number in Delhi, his hopes soaring with each ring, but a lump formed in his throat.

"Hello, who is this?" Balbir's familiar voice answered the phone. "Hello?" He frowned. "Hello? I cannot hear you."

Fear and uncertainty choked Chetan's words, leaving him unable to ask for Simran. With a heavy sigh, he hung up, lacking the courage to face the potential disappointment and rejection that awaited him. Every time he tried calling, it was always Balbir or Simran's mother who answered the phone, and he never dared to ask for her. Eventually, he stopped calling but still clung to the flicker of hope that their paths would cross again someday. The unspoken and unkept promises weighed heavy on his heart.

The year was 1994. A decade had passed since Operation Blue Star, the attack on the Golden Temple, the killing of Indira Gandhi, the Sikh massacre in Delhi, and the first time Chetan met Simran. Chetan was completely committed to pursuing his dreams. With Renu gone, Vikki busy in his college, and Vijay working in the office harder than ever, Chetan knew it was time for him to leave Patiala. He graduated from the engineering college and applied to various master's programs in US universities. He got accepted at almost all the colleges he applied to and was already dreaming about starting his new life in the United States. However, the US student visa was hard to secure. Chetan visited the embassy several times to get his visa, but it was denied every time.

"Not enough funds."

"Not enough ties to India."

"No clear career objectives."

These were the responses he received from the US consulate.

Chetan felt angry, frustrated, lost, and without any direction. He was convinced that no good could ever happen to him. He wanted to reach out to his father and garner some support, but Vijay was not the one who would help him and was always busy with his work. Chetan's ambition of going to the United States did not seem that important to him. He never asked what colleges Chetan was applying to or what specialization he wanted to do. Vijay remained aloof. After Renu's passing, he started spending even more time at his office, as if that were possible. Chetan was disappointed but determined not to give up. He decided to postpone his plans and try again in a few years after he had some work experience.

Chetan had to fall back on his plan B. He joined a company that had offered him an engineer trainee position through a campus interview. The job was in Delhi, and he decided to move there, hoping the new life would help him overcome the sense of failure and rejection. He got some new clothes stitched, got his luggage ready, and asked Vijay to arrange a car to bring him to his new place.

As he was traveling to Delhi, old memories began emerging. Suddenly, the failure of not getting to the United States did not seem so bad. A part of him was thankful that he did not go. There must be something better for him.

This must be my destiny, he thought as a strange excitement overtook him. This could be his opportunity to meet Simran again. He had a smile on his face.

Getting settled in the new job was relatively easy because the company provided accommodation and food. However, this was the first time Chetan lived outside his home, and he missed Vikki, his brother, and the comfort of the small town where everyone knew him. Delhi was too big of a city. People were not as warm, kept to themselves, and always seemed rushed. To Chetan, they looked like ants just running around with the single goal of living to get by another day. There seemed to be no other purpose in their lives.

I'll get out of here, he reminded himself.

I cannot live this nine-to-five life, working just to make a living. I want to live.

Chetan yearned for a life without self-doubts, without fear, where he could do what he wanted without hesitation. He wanted to travel, see new places, and have the courage to talk to strangers without being scared. He longed for the day when he would have his family back. He aspired to reach a day when he would become someone of certain consequence, admired by people and appreciated by loved ones.

Thoughts about Simran grew stronger. He wanted to meet her and pick things up from where they had left off. After months of deliberations and collecting some courage, Chetan thought of reaching out to Simran again.

What will she look like now? he wondered.

Will she recognize me? Will she even acknowledge knowing me? Will she be with someone else? All sorts of thoughts were coming to his mind.

What if I meet her and Balbir comes to know? What if they send some goons to beat me up? The menacing thoughts and fear would never leave him.

All these negative emotions were hounding his mind, ideas that had no grounding in reality. He had difficulty controlling his thoughts but had gotten used to pushing through them and carrying on. It was a painful process, but there was no other way he knew. Years of living in a traumatic environment and feeling unaccepted at home were ingrained deep into his psyche. Pulling up and forcing himself to finish the day's work became his arduous routine. Gathering all his strength, he finally decided to call Simran at the number he still remembered. He hoped they still had the same number. He eventually made the phone call.

"Hello?"

"…Hello, is Simran at home?" he finally asked.

"No, she is in the hospital. Who is this?" It was an older male voice on the other side. Chetan assumed it was Balbir. Chetan did not hang up the phone this time. He clutched the headset with all his strength and cleared his throat to speak up.

"*Sat Sri Akaal*, Uncle! This is her friend Chetan. What time will she be back?" Chetan took a chance, hoping he wouldn't get yelled at.

"She will be back by eight."

"Thank you. I'll try again." And he hung up. An adrenaline rush soaked his body; his heart was pounding hard, and his face was flushed red. Only he knew how much courage he had to summon to make this call. And then he waited until eight o'clock in the evening. He wanted to get this over with.

"Hello, is Simran home?" he asked, calling at eight sharp.

"Who is this?" This time, it was a female voice, younger.

"Chetan."

"Chetan? From Patiala?"

"Yes, I am Chetan from Patiala."

"Hi, Chetan, Simran here. How are you?"

Is she sad or disappointed? Chetan thought as he was expecting some more excitement in her response.

Does she not want to talk to me? He wondered.

"I am fine. How are you?"

"I am doing good. Where are you calling from?"

"I am here in Delhi. I work here now." Chetan kept his emotions under control. "So, you are a doctor now?"

"Almost. Finishing my residency," Simran said.

Chetan could feel her voice relaxing, and he imagined a smile on her face.

"Let's meet and catch up," Chetan gathered some courage and asked.

"Sure, let's meet up this Saturday. I am off," she replied without much hesitation. Again, not how Chetan expected this would go.

The three days leading up to Saturday were hard to pass. They were meeting at the newly opened KFC in the Defence Colony. It was the posh place where people would gather to experience the American way—one of the gifts of globalization. Chetan was prepping and rehearsing what he would wear, how he would open the conversation, and what he would say. He was not much of a small talker, and having conversations was hard for him, unlike Simran, who was a natural. Maybe he would just let her take the lead.

He was waiting inside the restaurant. He was early, as always. Paranoid about missing his meeting with Simran.

What if there is traffic, I get late, and she leaves before I arrive?

Soon, he saw a young woman in a pastel green *salwar kameez* opening the door. He stood up. It was her, even more beautiful now. She still had that silky brown hair tied in a single braid flowing to her hips. Her glowing skin needed no makeup. The soft lip color let her eyes shine and do their magic. Her fingers and toes were painted in a light shade of pink. She seemed so delicate, ethereal, as if floating toward him. He had a lump in his throat, wondering if he could even talk.

"Hey, Chetan! I can't believe it's really you!" she exclaimed. Her eyes shone, and a breathless expression of happiness radiated from her.

"I am doing good. You?" Chetan was relieved to see her excitement. He cleared his throat and extended his hand for a handshake.

She smiled with her eyebrows rising, questioning his handshake, and put her arms around him, hugging him. Chetan's arm was still extended. He slowly circled his arms around her and rested his head on her shoulder. He remembered that smell. She always had this subtle fragrance of rose. Chetan took a deep breath.

"It is so good to see you," Chetan began. He pointed to the chair.

Simran nodded and took a seat.

"So, how come you remembered me after all these years?"

"I never forgot you. You were always on my mind," Chetan blurted and then reconsidered his response. It was not the absolute truth, and the statement might have been too cheesy for Simran's taste. She was not into such conversations.

"Oh, really? Then how come you never called me?"

"I did. A few times. Did not get through to you."

"Hmm, I see."

"Well, Ms. Doctor. What kind of doctor are you?" Chetan tried his best to keep the conversation going.

"I am finishing my residency and will apply for an MD in psychiatry." She grinned.

Well, that's great! Chetan thought. He could certainly use a shrink by his side, since his head constantly needed fixing.

"I want to marry you." The words just jumped from his mouth. He regretted it immediately. He did not plan to say this in the very first meeting after seven years. He did not even know her that well.

"Oh, wow!" A loud laugh erupted. She was giggling, holding the side of her waist, and looking at the floor. Then, she pulled herself together and looked at him.

"I was just kidding." Chetan tried to pull back.

"No, you weren't." Simran was now even more amused. She was having a bit too much fun with the situation—more than Chetan liked.

"So, I assume you are ready to talk to my parents," she said, almost throwing it out as a challenge.

"Yes, absolutely!" Chetan was now smiling, getting the control back and continuing the jest.

"You know my father, right? He will eat you alive," Simran's eyes were now locked into his, as if she was trying to gauge his determination, to see how far he would go to get her.

"I am not afraid, Simran. I'd love to meet him." He did not smile this time.

"Okay, I'll think about it. But, for now, I am getting hungry."

"Oh, sorry. What would you like to have?"

Chetan came back home with a feeling of triumph. This was more than he expected of himself. He was smiling and laughing by himself. A sense of euphoria overtook him, a sensation that seldom came to him. He put on some music and sang along with it. He was in the moment and felt alive.

In the bustling city of Delhi, amid the winds of change and the whispers of a transforming nation, Chetan and Simran continued to meet. Their conversations flowed effortlessly, filled with laughter and dreams shared. As they spent more time together, their bond deepened, and they embarked on a delicate journey of love, secretly shielding their relationship from prying eyes, especially those of their parents. They met in hidden corners of the city, seeking refuge in crowded cafés and sometimes far from the crowds at Qutub Minar, where their love could bloom away from the watchful gaze of society. Beneath the shadows of ancient monuments and within the labyrinthine alleys of Old Delhi, they found solace and companionship.

Their relationship blossomed with stolen glances and moments as they navigated a world that still frowned upon such youthful love. They exchanged their hopes and fears, their dreams and aspirations. With each passing day, Chetan's love for Simran grew stronger, fueled by the determination to create a future where he could be with her openly, without fear. He dreamed of a world where love conquered everything and traditions, expectations, and the weight of past tragedies surrendered to the unyielding power of their connection.

Chetan was embarking on a new journey of defiance, bravery, and hope as he learned to navigate the treacherous realm of societal norms and potential parental disapproval, especially from Balbir Singh. This was a new chapter in Chetan's life that he was not used to, but the newfound courage was a welcome break from his worrying habits. For the first time in his life, he was living.

Chetan and Simran had been seeing each other for a while. Over three years. Simran had finished her MD and was now working in a hospital.

"Would you like to visit my home?" Simran brought it up one day.

"You mean to meet your parents?"

"Yes, I think it is about time," she said with gravity in her eyes. "They've started their search for grooms."

"Sure, if you are ready." Chetan did not want anything to come in the way of what he had with Simran. Disapproval from her parents meant an inevitable end of their relationship, but he knew he could not avoid them forever. The time had finally come.

Chetan fretted. Facing Balbir would be challenging. Knowing all the things Balbir and his family had gone through, a Hindu from outside their community asking for the hand of his most precious daughter would not be easy. He wondered if Balbir and his family hated him, his kind.

Chetan finally knocked at the door.

"*Sat Sri Akaal.* My name is Chetan," he said with his hands folded in front of his chest. He was looking at Balbir. The same red eyes as he remembered from the first and the only time he had met him.

Balbir just stood there, staring at him.

20

Chetan Malhotra

In 1999, Chetan eventually made it out of India, as he had always wanted. His search for safety, stability, and hopes for a fresh start, far from the shadows of the past, brought him to the West Coast of the United States of America. California offered it all: a career, comfortable lifestyle, higher standard of living, everything that symbolized success for Chetan.

Upon his arrival, he rented an apartment in Fremont. His office was in San Francisco, but Fremont was more affordable and boasted a sizable Indian community. Moreover, the nearby BART station offered an easy commute.

Chetan had been in the US for nearly three months. It was another routine day – he got ready for work, finished his blueberry muffin and a cup of milk with instant coffee. He walked to the Fremont BART station to board the Green Line 8:07 a.m. train toward San Francisco/Daly City, a forty-five-minute ride.

But today, an uneasiness overtook him as the BART train rattled and hummed toward the vibrant city of San Francisco.

Most passengers, lost in their thoughts or engrossed in their devices, seemed unaffected by the commute's usual commotion. However, amid this seemingly ordinary situation, Chetan couldn't help but feel a nervous discomfort.

He always sat near the middle of the train car, supposedly the safest place, and his eyes scanned each passenger as they boarded the train. The habit from the 1980s was deeply rooted in him. These train rides reminded him of the cautious journeys to his grandparents' house.

When the train stopped at the South Hayward station, a homeless person boarded. His disheveled appearance, tattered clothing, and worn-out backpack made Chetan slightly shift in his seat. His gut seemed to twist up, and his breath got shallow.

Murmurs of conversation faded to silence as the man took a seat a few rows before him. A gust of stale air swept in, carrying the heavy odor of unwashed clothes, forcing the three passengers sitting near him to vacate their seats and stand on the other end. Palms clammy, Chetan saw the wary glances exchanged among his fellow passengers. The impoverished man mumbled incoherently to himself and intermittently yelled, startling the passengers.

Chetan's mind spun out of control with a mix of fear and restlessness. He tried to force his thoughts from fear to sympathy for the person, yet an internal conflict churned within him.

Chetan closed his eyes, trying even harder not to think anything negative. He wanted the journey to end as soon as possible. Minutes turned into an eternity until, finally, the train approached Chetan's destination—the Montgomery BART station. As the doors opened and the passengers spilled onto the platform, Chetan rushed out and couldn't help but glance back at the man one last time. Chetan walked to the office, and his heart was racing unusually fast. He took the elevator to the twelfth floor, quickly got to his desk, and started his computer. The uneasiness was becoming more potent by the minute. He started experiencing shooting pains in his chest and arms, and drops of sweat were rolling down his temple.

I think I am having a heart attack. What should I do? Should I call the doctor?

Chetan was still new to the country and had no clue what options he had. He pulled out his medical card, which had a doctor's number. He decided to call.

"Thanks for calling the doctor's office. If this is a life-threatening emergency, please hang up and dial 9-11," came the automated message. Chetan waited for several minutes, and finally, a person responded.

"Hello, how can I help you?" asked the voice on the other side.

"I need to see a doctor. I am having chest pains, and my heart is beating really fast!"

"Sir, I suggest you go to an emergency room."

"Emergency?" This ratcheted up Chetan's panic. *Is this how I die?*

"Which hospital?" he asked, unfamiliar with the medical system in the US.

"Sir, any hospital. If it is a heart issue, the protocol is to go to the emergency."

Chetan hastily packed his bag and told his manager that he didn't feel well and needed to leave. Chetan hailed a taxi and went straight to the Saint Francis Memorial emergency room.

"Ram, Ram, Ram, Ram...." Chetan whispered the entire way

to the hospital.

The antiseptic scent hit his nose immediately as he rushed through the sliding doors of the emergency room. Chetan hurriedly approached the window.

"I need help," he stammered.

The harried attendant pushed a clipboard with some forms in front of him. "Fill these out, and we'll call you as soon as we can."

The reception area was crowded, with people having strained expressions, some moaning and clutching their paperwork.

This does not look like an ER. It is more of an outpatient department. Well, if I collapse here, there will be people to take care of me. All sorts of thoughts were going inside his head.

He waited about forty minutes, then a nurse called his name and ushered him through a maze of corridors into a small room. A narrow examination table, draped in crisp paper, stood at the room's center, surrounded by stainless steel cabinets stocked with medical supplies. She asked him to sit on the table and took his vitals.

"One thirty. Your heart is racing."

"Yes," said Chetan with a slight smile, trying to hide his fear.

"Let's do the EKG." The nurse hooked him to the machine.

Chetan looked at the device as it buzzed, generating the paper stream with line charts.

"How does it look?" he asked anxiously.

"Doctor will come and discuss with you."

And he waited another forty-five minutes.

"Hello, Mr. Malhotra. How are you doing?" the doctor asked, a warm smile on his face.

"I am feeling fine," Chetan replied.

"Well, everything looks fine. We'll send the report to your doctor. Go and see him when you get a chance."

That's it? Well, that was a bit underwhelming. At least it was not a heart attack.

The following day, Chetan visited his doctor.

"So, Mr. Malhotra, what brings you in today?" Dr. Miller asked.

Chetan described this whole ordeal at the most extraordinary lengths.

"Seems you had a panic attack," the doctor said. "Work stressful lately?"

Chetan had never heard the term "panic attack" before. It would take him a few more visits to the emergency rooms before he started recognizing them and learning to manage them.

Chetan's life bore the weight of a turbulent past that had left indelible scars on his spirit. His mind often wandered into the tumultuous years of the 1980s, which engulfed Punjab in violence and political turmoil. He remembered the ominous atmosphere that had pervaded his neighborhood, the constant fear of death that hung in the air like a heavy cloud. He still carried the weight of fear and anger he felt growing up in a stressful home that proved to be more than a dark phase and became the crucible that shaped the rest of his life. The memories of those days surrounded Chetan's mind like a never-ending nightmare he desperately wanted to wake from.

Still, the harder he tried to escape it, the deeper he sank.

The slightest reminders of the violence he had witnessed would trigger another panic episode. The sound of a car backfiring, the sight of a crowded street, or even the smell of smoke could transport him back to those terrifying days in

Punjab. Each panic attack was a relic of the scars from his past that could not be erased.

His need to protect and control each aspect of his life kept turning compulsive. He needed to safeguard his family, relationships, reputation, and everything he felt he lost during childhood. He did not want to make any "silly mistakes." He lived in constant fear of some misfortune lurking somewhere in the corner that would pounce on his every happiness. Every step out of the house seemed a burden. Every time he drove his car, he feared getting into an accident. He would pray when he crossed any bridge lest it should collapse. He would pray if he walked under a bridge in case it might crumble. Whenever he took his plane seat, he had a strong urge to exit immediately. He would look at the flight attendants closing the door, hoping they would cancel the flight and let him outside. He would shut his eyes, trying to force himself to sleep, feeling jealous of people who could sip wine and work on their laptops on planes so nonchalantly. Every achievement seemed transient, and every pleasure short-lived and only there to lure him into tragedy. He was incapable of any celebration. All birthdays seemed a burden, all accomplishments forewarning of some loss. The feeling that something dreadful was about to happen would never leave Chetan.

He kept checking, rearranging, and organizing all aspects of his life to get control, to get it into a predictable structure. But, on the contrary, he became a prisoner of his rituals, and his obsessions and compulsions became severe. In his quest to seek order, Chetan would spend hours each day orienting his workspace and personal belongings, ensuring everything was lined up in a specific arrangement. Shoes had to be kept parallel on the floor. If the floor had squares, his shoes could not touch the boundary of those squares. While walking, he could not step on any lines. It was funny to watch him hopping over the lines of the sidewalk. When he saw an airplane in the sky, he would fold his hands in prayer and wish the passengers a safe landing. He counted everything in his head: sips of his coffee, bites from his plate, the number of times he chewed his food before he swallowed. He kept relocking the door dozens of times before he would feel convinced enough to leave his house.

Chetan was aware of his odd behavior and dealt with frustration and embarrassment. He often felt ashamed of all the rituals he practiced to gain control over his surroundings. But he couldn't help it. The years of darkness had a firm hold on him. It was not something he could think away. One cannot easily forget the experiences growing up in the shadows of death and fear. The anxiety and discomfort he felt when things were out of place were overwhelming, and he felt like he had no choice but to feed his compulsive behaviors.

At work, Chetan spent hours cleaning and organizing his office, wiping down his desk, and managing his files and documents. He would get anxious if anyone came into his office and touched his things. He would spend hours rehearsing his speeches, detailing slides, and memorizing essential lines. But, as the time to deliver approached, Chetan would feel his palms sweating and a vice squeezing out every drop of blood from his heart. He struggled to control his breath. Lightheaded and dizzy, he could barely stave off the urge to run away and hide.

Chetan had been in the US for eight years now. He had built a life for himself far away from Punjab. He had moved, hoping to leave behind the ghosts of his past. But, despite the physical distance, his mind remained tethered to those harrowing memories. That darkness manifested itself frequently as anxiety; it was a cruel reminder that his traumatic past still held power over him. His triumphs were well recognized; however, there was also darkness inside him that he kept hidden from people. The trauma he had endured in his formative years continued to haunt him, even in his newfound home.

Pushing through all his fears, he kept rising to become a top executive at one of the biggest tech companies in the valley. He worked with some of the industry's brightest and most innovative people, full of confidence and aggression that he found hard to master. His doubts often resurfaced.

What if I make a fool of myself?

How could a simpleton from a small town in Punjab deserve to be here?

How would I work with all these brilliant people?

The fear of exposing himself was constant and exhausting. However, Chetan was becoming increasingly aware of such overpowering feelings. He recognized them and accepted them as something he had to live with. Sometimes, he would laugh when those thoughts arrived to see if they would leave him alone. Chetan reminded himself that he was strong and capable and could handle anything that came his way.

Wasn't I able to overcome so many adversities to reach this point?

He would forcibly pull himself out of the darkness, trying to distract himself with some happy thoughts.

Chetan managed his professional life with humility and poise. He had learned to mask his anxiety, present himself as a calm, composed executive, and be productive. The boy who once cowered in fear at the slightest incident grew into a stronger person, his spirit unyielding in the face of adversity. He learned to recognize the early signs and devised coping strategies.

However, it took a significant toll on his mental well-being.

The year 1984, the height of the terrorism in Punjab, was now more than twenty years ago, but the haunting memories of those dark times still lingered, plaguing his mind and tormenting his soul. His childhood was overshadowed by the constant threat of violence, bomb blasts, and the ever-present danger lurking in the streets. The turbulent political climate had cast a dark shadow over the entire region, and everyone, including Chetan's family, lived in constant fear. The implications reverberated globally and still do so today. Chetan grew up in an atmosphere that no child should ever endure. He had seen innocent lives being torn apart, heard the deafening sound of explosions, and felt a palpable fear in the air. Those early experiences had etched themselves deeply, and Chetan was left to confront them every waking hour.

Despite his struggles, Chetan was determined to succeed. He wanted to be better than his father. He worked to become more successful and a better man than Vijay. His anxiety would not hold him back from experiencing unfamiliar things, exploring new places, and meeting strangers. After all, that was the life he was looking for. It was the reason he left India. He refused to let his anxiety and panic attacks control his life.

He tried every possible way to get control. He visited doctors, consulted psychiatrists, and pursued a journey of therapy and medication to cope with his anxiety. Still, the specter of the 1980s continued to cast a long shadow over his life. Prescription drugs provided temporary respite, allowing him to regain control over his debilitating symptoms. However, as time went on, Chetan began to resent his reliance on medication to manage his panic attacks and anxiety. He reverted to his old ways of slogging through challenging situations and devising new coping mechanisms.

In the depths of his darkest moments, Chetan found himself wondering about the concept of death. Not out of a desire to end his life but somewhat as a means of overcoming his fear of mortality. A human born in this world has to die one day, so why worry about it? He imagined death as a gateway to a new existence, one where he would be reborn as a stronger, more courageous individual—a person unburdened by the shackles of anxiety. Chetan developed a peculiar fascination to understand the mystery of death. The thought that scared him suddenly started to bring a feeling of relief. The acceptance of mortality comforted him and helped him live in the moment. He found a peculiar element of beauty in death. He would close his eyes and think of eventual escape as a doorway to something beyond the confines of his mortal realm, to a place where pain and suffering have no room. He would imagine what it would be like to shed the physical body's limitations and embrace an expansive, spiritual existence.

The aesthetic quality of death fascinated Chetan, but he found his intrigue challenging to articulate. Perhaps for him, it was the finality of it all, the sense that everything that came before would have one moment of closure. He imagined a time when all the pain, suffering, anxiety, and fear would vanish. All past pain and sorrow, the death and destruction he grew up with, would one day melt away. The loss Chetan witnessed and endured was profound and frequently left him adrift in the past. But, in that grief, he looked for a sense of connection that would help him to mourn and reconcile with the past. He imagined being reincarnated as a much stronger human with the courage and control to lead life decisively.

Accepting that time on this earth is limited helped Chetan better appreciate the beauty and wonder of the world. He embraced the fleeting nature of existence and tried to find beauty in the moments that make up our lives–reminding himself that suffering is not forever but merely a transition to something more beautiful and everlasting. The ephemeral nature of life was something he started to enjoy, and he found comfort in knowing that nothing lasts forever. He was amused at long-term planning meetings.

When anyone would ask him about his long-term goals, Chetan would quote Keynes to everyone's dismay: "In the long run, we are all dead."

While he devised ways to overcome his anxiety, it was abundantly clear to him that the decade of 1980 was not a chapter that he could close. The wounds remained unhealed, the scars running deep.

Despite the distance between him and the past, the trauma of those dark days continued to trouble him as he remained tangled in the legacy of 1984.

21

Home

The Independence Day crowd in Fremont started to dwindle, the floats long gone. Many stalls were in the process of dismantling their booths. People were picking up their chairs and walking to the parking lots. The sun in the clear blue sky made the day unusually warm. The slow breeze that had picked up some cooling air from Lake Elizabeth was a welcome reprieve from the hot sun. Chetan loved this weather. He loved going to the lake and jogging around its perimeter. He had taken on running as a way to manage his anxiety and panic attacks. One lap around the lake was two miles. He would do five laps every weekend.

Chetan had been living in Fremont for eight years now. He thought he had left behind the land that reminded him of the scars of 1984 and his childhood wounds. Although, on this day, looking at the demonstrations and protests, those memories would return. The memories of bus killings, bomb blasts, traveling terrified, Vijay's carpool, the Delhi massacre, and the murder of students at his college. With that feeling, more reminders of childhood trauma would surface. Chetan remembered his mother's frustration, his father's indifference, their fights, and beatings at home. He thought about Renu, whose sickness and sudden death left him and his family in disarray. Were they responsible for her death? Did they give her a chance to survive? What if they could have taken her to a better hospital and diagnosed her early on? Maybe she would still be with them.

After Renu's death, Vijay and the two boys had to pull themselves together. There was not much time for grieving. Chetan thought about young Vikki, who was confused and felt lost after Mom's death. With Chetan at college and Vijay busy with work, Vikki had to figure out the course of his life on his own. With no counseling tools available at the time to diagnose what was happening inside their heads, work was the only coping mechanism they relied on.

Well, I left Punjab but brought all the pain with me, he thought and smiled.

Chetan thought about his father. He could have remarried but did not. Chetan wondered if he should have even been married in the first place. Vijay was not a person who had much attachment to any relationship. He was kind and honest. However, he never took the role of a strong patriarch who could protect his family, guide his family, or put the family's interests ahead of his work. He sacrificed a lot for his work, almost every time, at the cost of his family. Chetan wondered if Vijay ever realized that, despite Renu's constant displeasure and loud fights.

Chetan thought about his father's aloofness. His contribution to building and bringing up a family was almost negligible. Sometimes, Chetan wondered how he grew up in that broken home to be what he was today. But he knew that despite all his success, there was a lot of scar tissue. Deep down, his paranoia, overcautiousness, and obsession to organize were deeply rooted in growing up in that household in the eighties in Punjab. He always wondered if there were more like him—the silent sufferers. On the surface, they seemed lucky to escape those times unscathed, but underneath, were they undergoing undiagnosed post-traumatic stress disorder?

In the weaning crowds, he could visualize survivors of domestic abuse, people who survived the atrocities of the police, who had escaped the burning cities, left their lives behind or lost their loved ones. He imagined their stories, feeling their pain and admiring their courage. They all were heroes. He marveled at human resilience. He wondered about the strength they needed to pick themselves up and make it to the shores of the United States, thousands of miles from home. The words of Emma Lazarus echoed in Chetan's ears: "Give me your tired, your poor, / Your huddled masses yearning to breathe free, / The wretched refuse of your teeming shore." Yes, the wretched refuse they all were. Some had suffered through generations to finally build a home for themselves. Many journeys to the US shore were not as smooth as Chetan's. Walking days through the desert, through snow, or huddled in transport containers, in car trunks—they all had a story to tell. They tried and failed repeatedly but somehow kept moving to find the land of the free.

His thoughts drifted to Balbir, wondering if Balbir would join the demonstrations today. Did these people today represent him? Balbir was driven out of his home twice, first during the partition of newly independent India, when his childhood was cut short. He lost his brother, his family, his wealth, and his innocence. And then, a second time during the Delhi riots, he had to flee to save his family, his dignity, and his life. How did Balbir feel when Raju had to cut his hair, Chetan wondered. The symbol of honor that was sacrificed to save his life. It must have killed him from within. He was an honest businessman and stayed far away from any politics. So, how did he get entangled in all the devastation? Was he just collateral damage when big political egos clashed?

Chetan was different from Balbir. He would not even compare his hardships to what Balbir underwent. Although, in a way, Chetan was a survivor as well. From the outside, Chetan was a symbol of success, the American dream coming true, but from the inside, he was fighting many demons. He moved far away from places that reminded him of his pain and built a home for himself. But Balbir returned to the place that had inflicted the most pain on him to fight for what was rightfully his. Chetan admired his strength, his conviction.

However, Chetan did not have the same regard for Vijay. Their relationship was cordial. They cared for each other, but Vijay's shortcomings were too much for Chetan to ignore. Renu's words were engraved in his mind: "Don't be like your father." He promised himself he would be a better husband and a better father. But how far can an apple fall from the tree? To his dismay, he was becoming more and more like his father. Overcommitted to work, finding it hard to find any joy outside of work. At times, Chetan would get disgusted by his own behavior, his becoming Vijay. He fought hard to unlearn the instincts the years of upbringing had instilled in him. The family was essential to Chetan, and he kept reminding himself of that. His mental struggles continued; mental episodes would come and go, and he would live to fight another day, pushing himself through the challenges, rising through the ranks of corporate America, and trying to keep his home intact.

The park was now almost empty. The protesters were gone. Some black flags were lying on the ground as a lingering reminder of decades of pain and suffering. The grand marshal of the parade was whisked away to a VIP lunch-cum-fundraiser for an Indian-American candidate planning to run for Congress. Volunteers picked up trash in large black plastic bags, only to prepare the grounds for another day of plundering and garbage dumping.

Just like my life, Chetan thought.

Among those volunteers was the same woman who was serving tea. She still had the same energy as she had a few hours back. Chetan was in awe of her strength and calmness. Even after staying among the agitated crowd for hours, she was still gentle. Not even once did she stop serving or raise an eyebrow. Her servitude was evenly dedicated to both sides. Her commitment to *seva* was unwavering. It did not discriminate based on caste, religion, race, or wealth. It did not matter who was in front of her; she was acting out of her duty and being true to herself.

Chetan rose and began cleaning the area around him. Doing his part, he grabbed a black trash bag from the volunteer booth and started picking up the used paper cups and plates lying on the ground. Cups of tea, water, and food plates were scattered everywhere, despite there being trash cans all around.

"Why can we Indians not keep public places clean? Why is it so hard for us?" he muttered to himself. Chetan felt his annoyance growing, but he kept it tamed and focused on cleaning up. He counted as he picked up discarded objects, an involuntary urge to count every action.

"One, two, three, four . . ." he continued. To others, he must appear to be a grumpy recluse mumbling to himself, but he was just a prisoner of his rituals. Chetan filled up a few bags quickly. He had the habit of creating competition out of anything. He had to be the fastest, filling the most bags, and he wanted people to acknowledge that. With each bag stacked, he would look at others to see if they noticed. How efficient he was compared to them. He was the best trash picker among them. Was it the need to be the best or the desire to get praise from others, to be encouraged? Something he did not get from Renu or Vijay growing up.

That woman in the yellow kurta and blue jeans with the *dupatta* on her head had also finished her cleanup. She was thanking all the volunteers, her hands clasped together. She was neither looking for any praise nor doing it for any recognition. Her only purpose was to be the glue, trying ever so hard to unite the community. Every year, she was there, serving people from all sides, all religions, and all backgrounds, without any reservations.

Eventually, she turned, and her eyes stopped at Chetan, standing some fifty feet away. She stood there and looked at him as if some old memories had stopped her in her tracks. Chetan gave her a quick glance and then dropped his head, eyes looking at the ground, trying to hide his face. Then, after some effort, he raised his head again. His mouth was getting dry. The woman adjusted her *dupatta* one more time and started walking toward him.

Chetan's heartbeat was rising. His face was flush, and his ears got warmer. He was mesmerized by her gait as she approached him. He was struggling with conflicting feelings. He wanted to be with her and keep admiring her from a distance.

She stood before him, looking up with a straight, strong posture. Their eyes locked. Chetan was getting weak in his knees.

"Chetan, what's wrong?" Simran asked.

"Nothing." He looked into her eyes, trying his hardest not to look away.

"Are you okay?" she asked again.

"Yes, I'll be fine."

"Will be fine? Haan?"

"You know what I mean, Simran. Let's get to our house."

"I do. And it is called our home!" She held his hands in hers and pulled him away.

"Yes. Home."

Chetan smiled and grabbed her hand tight. Tighter than usual. It still felt like the first time he held her hand in the class. So soft yet strong. So small yet could fit his whole world.

"Your hands are sweaty," she said softly, teasing him.

"You can let it go."

"Never," she declared, looking straight into his eyes.

TIKI BEACH

PARADISE CRIME COZY MYSTERY #6

TOBY NEAL